'I like you, Remy. But I can't see you as anything more than the boy I used to play with.'

'I don't believe you.' Remy was scathing. 'You've just had second thoughts, that's all.'

'No.' Megan couldn't believe she was having this conversation with him. 'Please…you know your mother would be so upset if she knew what was going on…'

'My mother!' Remy said the words almost contemptuously. 'Are you afraid we're going to offend her? My God, it's been a long time since I allowed my mother to make any decisions in my life.'

Megan moved her head from side to side. 'Remy…'

'What?'

She edged towards the door. 'This is crazy.'

'I agree.' But instead of abandoning the argument he closed the space between them. Cupping her hot face between his palms, he looked down at her with dark intent. 'This isn't anything to do with anyone else. It's to do with us, that's all. With the fact that you want me as much as I want you.'

Anne Mather began writing when she was a child, progressing through torrid teenage romances to the kind of adult romances she likes to read. She's married, with two children, and lives in the north of England. After writing, she enjoys reading, driving, and travelling to different places to find settings for new novels. She considers herself very lucky to do something that she not only enjoys, but also gets paid for.

SINFUL PLEASURES

BY
ANNE MATHER

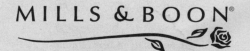
MILLS & BOON®

*First published in Great Britain 1998
Harlequin Mills & Boon Limited,
Eton House, 18-24 Paradise Road, Richmond, Surrey TW9 1SR*

© Anne Mather 1998

ISBN 0 263 80735 5

*Set in Times Roman 10 on 10¾ pt.
01-9804-58224 C1*

*Printed and bound in Great Britain
by Mackays of Chatham PLC, Chatham*

CHAPTER ONE

IT HAD been snowing when she left London. Great fat flakes that brushed against the aircraft's windows and covered the runway in a feathery coat of white. She had wondered if the plane would be able to take off in such conditions; or perhaps she had hoped that it wouldn't, she reflected tautly. Then she would have had a legitimate excuse for staying at home.

And it wasn't as if she didn't like the snow, she assured herself. It was much more the sort of weather she was used to at this time of the year. A blazing sun and blue-green seas were out of place in January, even if the shops back home were already anticipating the holiday season ahead.

Not everyone would agree with her, of course; she knew that. Indeed, most people would consider the opportunity to spend four weeks in the Caribbean a godsend. Particularly in her circumstances, she conceded. After a miserable Christmas spent in a hospital bed.

But most people were not her, Megan reminded herself impatiently, shifting somewhat uneasily in the comfortable aircraft seat. She didn't want to be going to the Caribbean, in good health or in bad. She had no incipient longings to see her so-called stepfather and his family again. Since her mother died, she had had little or no contact with the Robards, and that had suited her very well. Very well indeed.

Below the aircraft, the turquoise waters mocked her feelings. Whether she wanted it or not, she was now less than an hour from her destination. Already the huge jet was beginning its descent towards Cap Saint Nicolas, and the island of San Felipe would soon be beneath them. However reluctant she might be to renew her acquaintance with her mother's second family, it was no longer an option. By stepping aboard the aircraft, she had taken any alternative out of her hands.

It was a small consolation that it had not been entirely her decision. The fact that her stepsister had phoned while she was still in the hospital had been pure chance. Simon had answered the call, knowing nothing of the rift that had developed between herself and the Robards. He had had no hesitation in telling Anita that Megan was ill; had probably exaggerated her illness, in fact, as he was prone to do; and he had thought Anita was being kind when she had suggested Megan might like to spend a few weeks with them to recuperate. It had never occurred to him that she might not want to go.

And, of course, Anita was being kind, Megan acknowledged ruefully. Anita had always been kind, and in other circumstances their friendship might have survived. Anita was much older, but she had always treated the younger girl with affection. After all, if it hadn't been for Anita and Remy, Megan would have found those holidays spent with her mother and the man who was to become her stepfather very lonely indeed.

But, even so, she would never have accepted Anita's invitation in the ordinary way. Her stepsister might have issued the invitation, but Megan knew she wouldn't have done so without her father's consent. Ryan Robards probably controlled his daughter now, just as he had done all those years ago. If Megan was coming to San Felipe, it was because it suited Ryan Robards that she should.

The trouble was, it didn't suit her, Megan thought frustratedly. And now that she was actually nearing her destination she couldn't imagine how she had allowed herself to be persuaded to come. But her illness, and the weakness it had engendered, had left her susceptible to Simon's inducements. She needed a break, he had told her firmly. And where better than with people who cared about her?

Only they didn't care about her, she protested silently. Not really. Not the grown-up woman she had become. They remembered Meggie, the child, the fifteen-year-old adolescent. The girl who had been naïve enough to think that her parents would never get a divorce.

Megan sighed, and adjusted the pillow behind her head yet again, drawing the attention of the ever vigilant stewardess. 'Can I get you anything, Ms Cross?' she enquired, her smile warm and solicitous, and Megan forced herself to answer in the same unassuming tone.

'No, thanks,' she replied, wishing she could ask for a large Scotch over ice, with a twist of lemon for good measure. But the medication she was still obliged to take denied any use of alcohol, and she was sufficiently considerate of the tenderness of her stomach not to take any risks.

The stewardess went away again and Megan tried to relax. After all, that was what she was here for. To relax; to get away from phones and faxes, and the never-ending demands of the designer directory she and Simon Chater had founded almost eight years ago. Work had become her life, her obsession. Nothing else had seemed so important. Not possessions, not people, and most especially not her health.

The ironic thing was, she didn't honestly see how coming to San Felipe was going to help her to relax. On the contrary, even the thought that they'd be landing shortly set her nerves on edge. Nothing Anita had said had convinced Megan that her stepfather would be pleased to see her. So far as Ryan Robards was concerned, she had betrayed her mother by choosing to live with her father. And even though Giles Cross was dead, too, the bitterness he'd suffered lived on.

The only optimistic note was that Anita had phoned without being aware that Megan was ill. After years, when their only contact had been through Christmas and birthday cards, she had called totally out of the blue. Even now, Megan wasn't precisely sure why Anita had phoned. Unless the goodwill of Christmas had inspired a sudden need to renew old ties.

But it was going to be difficult even so. Megan had no idea what she would say to someone she hadn't had a proper conversation with for more than sixteen years. How could she share her problems with a virtual stranger? She didn't even know if the other woman was married, let alone what might have happened to her son.

Remy.

Megan tilted her head against the cushioned rest and sighed. It was strange to think that Remy would be grown up, too. He'd been—what? Five? Six?—when she'd last seen him? A dark-haired little boy, who'd run around half naked most of the time, and who had taken a delight in teasing his older playmate: herself.

She hadn't asked Anita about Remy when she'd spoken to her. She'd been tense and uncommunicative, too intent on trying to find excuses why she shouldn't come to show any interest in Anita's affairs. Not that that had deterred her stepsister, she acknowledged. Anita had probably thought that Megan's attitude was the result of the weeks she'd spent under medication. She'd been adamant that Megan should come to San Felipe to regain her strength. It was what Megan's mother would have wanted, she'd insisted, and Megan couldn't argue with that.

She was getting more and more edgy, and, deciding she needed to reassure herself that she didn't look as sick as she felt, she took herself off to the toilet. In the narrow confines of the cubicle, she examined her pale features critically. Lord, she thought ruefully, it would take more than a re-application of her lipstick to give her face any life.

The truth was, she had been neglecting herself recently. But with Simon spending so much time in New York, organising the launch of the directory there, she had naturally had a lot more work to cope with. She should delegate more; she knew that. Simon was always telling her so. But she liked to feel that she was needed. A hang-up from her childhood, she supposed.

She leaned towards the mirror. Was that a grey hair? she wondered anxiously. Certainly, the fine strand glinted silver among the corn-silk helmet of hair that framed her face.

She shook her head and the offending hair disappeared, absorbed by the bell-like curve that cupped her chin.

Did she look too severe? she fretted, smoothing damp palms over the long narrow lines of her jacket. The trouser suit, with its fine cream stripe, was navy blue and not really a holiday outfit. She'd known Simon didn't approve of her choice from the minute she'd come downstairs that morning.

But she couldn't have worn something light and feminine, she told herself, not in her present state of mind. The navy suit was smart, if a trifle impersonal, and it was certainly more in keeping with her mood.

Someone tried the toilet door, reminding her that she was spending far too long analysing her appearance. What did it matter what she looked like, after all? She grimaced. She could be stopping someone from keeping an intimate assignation. As unlikely as it seemed, such things did go on.

Outside, the purser gave her a searching look. 'All right, Ms Cross?' he asked, his cheeky grin proving that he was not above having such thoughts about her. 'We'll be landing in a few minutes. If you'll take your seat and fasten your seatbelt, we'll soon have you safely on the ground.'

'Oh—good.' Megan managed a polite smile in return, and groped her way back to her seat. The aircraft was banking quite steeply now, and it was difficult to keep her balance. She put the sudden sense of nausea she felt down to a momentary touch of air-sickness.

Yet she guessed her feelings was mostly psychosomatic. The prospect of seeing the Robards again was what was really causing her concern. She wondered if her stepfather would come to the airport to meet her. What on earth was she going to say to him that wouldn't sound abysmally insincere?

Her stomach dropped suddenly, but this time it really was the effects of the plane levelling out before landing. The pilot lowered the undercarriage as they passed over the rocky promontory of Cap Saint Nicolas, and then they dipped towards the runway that ran parallel to the beach.

It was beautiful, she thought reluctantly as memories of the holidays she had spent here sent a painful thrill through her veins. She had been so naïve in those days; so innocent. Which was why she'd been so hurt when the truth had come out.

But she didn't want to think about that now. That period of her life was dead and gone—like her parents, she reflected bitterly. It was no use believing that her father would still be alive if her mother hadn't betrayed him; no good wondering if Laura—her mother—would have developed that obscure kind of skin cancer if she'd continued to live as his wife...

The plane landed without incident and taxied slowly towards the airport buildings. Megan remembered that when she'd first come here the formalities had been dealt with in a kind of Nissen hut, with a corrugated-iron roof that drummed noisily when it rained. And it did rain sometimes, she recalled unwillingly. Heavy, torrential rain that left the vegetation green and the island steaming.

But now, when the plane door was opened, and her fellow passengers began to disembark, Megan felt the heat almost before she stepped out onto the gantry. She was immediately conscious of the unsuitability of her clothes, and her skin prickled beneath the fine cashmere.

Consequently, she was glad to descend the steps, cross the tarmac, and step into the arrivals hall. Gladder still to discover that air-conditioning had also been installed, and the debilitating heat was left outside.

All the same, for once she wished she hadn't travelled first-class. On this occasion, being at the front of the queue that was forming had little appeal. She would have preferred to hang back, to let the rest of the passengers disperse before she collected her luggage. She was uneasily aware of how ill-prepared for this meeting she was.

Beyond Passport Control, the building opened out into the customs area. Two carousels were already starting to unload luggage from the British Airways plane. She saw, to her dismay, that her suitcases had already been unloaded, and, realising she was only delaying the inevitable, she went to claim them as hers.

She didn't know whether to feel glad or sorry when she emerged from the customs channel to find that neither Ryan nor Anita was waiting for her. She had acquired a porter to transport her luggage to where taxis traditionally touted for fares, but she hadn't considered that she might have to hire one herself.

She didn't know what to do. Her formal clothes set her apart from the regular holidaymakers, most of whom were dressed in lightweight summer gear. She looked more like a returning resident, she reflected. If only she'd had her own car in the car park.

The heat was really getting to her now. Even beneath the canopy that jutted out over the taxi rank, the moist air was sapping what little strength she had. On top of which, the porter she'd hired was beginning to get restless. Megan guessed he was thinking of all the gratuities he was missing, hanging about with her.

'Megan.'

The voice was unfamiliar, but he evidently knew her name, and she turned to give the man an enquiring look. Perhaps Ryan Robards employed a chauffeur these days, she reflected, regarding him with some reserve. In faded jeans and a skin-tight vest, with a single gold earring threaded through the lobe of his left ear, he didn't look the type of person to win anyone's confidence.

'Are you speaking to me?' she asked, somewhat stiffly, wondering if he was some kind of beach bum who haunted the airport looking for gullible tourists to fleece. Her eyes dropped to the suitcases on the porter's cart, suspecting he had got her name from the labels, but all her secretary had done was put 'Ms M Cross' on the tabs.

'It is Megan, isn't it?' he asked, tawny eyes mirroring his slight amusement at her formal response, and she realised he wasn't about to go away. On the contrary, he was watching her with intense interest, and she suddenly wished that Ryan Robards would appear.

'What if it is?' she asked now, glancing somewhat impatiently about her. For God's sake, she thought, where was Anita? Didn't she know what time the plane was due to land?

'Because I've come to meet you,' the man said coolly, and a look of consternation crossed her face. He handed the porter a couple of notes and plucked her cases from the trolley. 'If you'll come with me, the car's parked just along here.'

'Wait a minute.' Megan knew she was probably being far too cautious, but she couldn't just go with him without knowing who he was. 'I mean—I still don't know who you are,' she added uncertainly, licking her lips. 'Did Mr Robards send you? I expected—Anita—to come herself.'

The man sighed. He was still holding her cases, and she knew they must be heavy for him. Not that it seemed to bother him. His arms and shoulders looked sleekly muscular, the sinews rippling smoothly beneath honey-gold skin.

'I guess you could say they—sent me,' he agreed, at last, inclining his head with its unruly mane of night-dark hair. For a moment there was something vaguely familiar about his lean features, but she would still have preferred to send him on his way.

He started along the walkway and she had, perforce, to follow him. Either that, or say goodbye to her luggage, she decided, with some resignation. Besides, although it was after four o'clock, the sun was showing no signs as yet of weakening, and she was longing to get out of her formal clothes.

She was hot and sticky by the time they reached the car, though the fact that it was a long, low estate car, the closed windows hinting of air-conditioning, was some consolation. 'You get in,' the man suggested, a quick glance in her direction ascertaining that she was already wilting with fatigue. He flipped up the tailgate. 'I'll be with you in a minute. Mom guessed you'd prefer the Audi to the buggy.'

Megan blinked. 'Mom?' she echoed, gazing at him in

disbelief, and her companion permitted her a rueful grin. 'You're—Remy?' she gasped weakly, feeling in need of some support. 'My God!' She swallowed. 'I'm sorry. I had no idea.'

'No.' There was a faintly ironic twist to his lips as he responded. 'Welcome to San Felipe, *Aunt* Megan. I hope you're going to enjoy your stay.'

Megan blinked and then, realising she was staring at him with rather more curiosity than sense, she hastily folded her length into the car. But, 'Remy!' she breathed to herself, casting an incredulous look over her shoulder at the young man loading her suitcases into the back of the vehicle. She'd expected him to have grown up, but she'd never expected—never expected—

What?

She shook her head a little impatiently. What had she expected, after all? That the boy she remembered should have lost that lazy teasing humour? That he couldn't have turned into the attractive man she'd just met?

Nevertheless, she wouldn't have recognised him if he hadn't spoken. It was hard to associate the child she remembered with the man. He'd been little more than a baby when her mother had first brought her to San Felipe. It made her feel incredibly old suddenly. He'd called her 'Aunt' Megan, and she supposed that was what she was to him.

She wondered what he did for a living. Whether he worked for his grandfather at the hotel. There was the marina, too, of course, and an estate that grew coffee and fruit. He could probably have his choice of occupations. Just because he dressed like—like he did, that was no reason to assume he spent his time bumming around.

The tailgate slammed and presently Remy swung open the driver's door and got in beside her. Megan permitted him a rueful smile as he started the engine, but she was uncomfortably aware that her feelings weren't as uncomplicated as his.

'I recognised you,' he remarked, checking his rear-view

mirror before pulling out. 'I did,' he averred, when she looked disbelieving. 'You haven't changed that much. Apart from your hair, that is. You used to wear it long.'

So she had. Megan had to steel herself not to check her reflection in the vanity mirror. Her hair had always been straight, and in those days she'd used to curl it. By the time she was a teenager, it had been a frizzy mop.

'I don't know whether to regard that as a compliment,' she remarked now, grateful for the opening. 'God, I used to look such a fright in those days. And I was about twenty pounds overweight.'

'But not now,' observed Remy, his tawny eyes making a brief, but disturbing, résumé of her figure. 'Mom told us all about the operation. Imagine having ulcers at twenty-eight.'

'I'm almost thirty-one actually,' said Megan quickly, not quite sure why it was so necessary for her to state her age. 'And it wasn't ulcers, just one rather nasty individual. I'd been having treatment for it, but it didn't respond.'

'And it perforated.'

Megan nodded. 'Yes.'

'Mom said it was touch-and-go for a few hours.' He paused. 'Your boyfriend gave her all the gory details.'

'Did he?' Megan was about to explain that Simon wasn't her boyfriend, and then changed her mind. They did share a house, because it was convenient for both of them to do so. But anything else—well, that was their business and no one else's.

'Yeah.' Remy pulled out into the stream of traffic leaving the airport, his lean hands sliding easily around the wheel. 'I guess your job must stress you out. You need to learn to relax.'

Like you?

Megan pressed her lips together, turning to look out of the window to distract her eyes from his muscled frame. Dear God, she thought, who'd have thought that Anita's son would turn out to be such a hunk? If he ever got tired of island life, she could get him a modelling job in a minute.

Yet that wasn't really fair, she acknowledged, noticing that the road from the airport into the town of Port Serrat was now a dual carriageway. Remy might be a hunk, but he didn't possess the bland good looks of the models she'd dealt with. There was character in his lean features, and a rugged hardness about his mouth. The camera might love him, but she doubted he'd give it a chance.

In fact, he looked a lot like his grandfather, she thought with tightening lips. Ryan Robards had possessed the same raw sexuality that was so evident in his grandson. Of course, Remy might resemble his father, too, but that was something that had never been talked about, not in her presence anyway. She only knew that Anita had been little more than a schoolgirl herself when he was born.

'So what do you think of the old place?' he asked now, casting a glance in her direction, and Megan forced her disturbing memories aside. She hadn't come here to speculate about his parentage, even if her father had used that in his arguments more than once.

'It's—beautiful,' she said, and she meant it. The blur of white beaches and lush vegetation she had seen from the air had resolved itself into the colourful landscape she remembered. Between the twin carriageways, flowering shrubs and vivid flamboyants formed an exotic median, and away to her left the shimmering waters of Orchid Bay glistened in the sun. 'I always loved coming here.'

'So why have you stayed away?' asked Remy flatly, and then, as if realising that was a moot point, he went on, 'I know Mom's looking forward to seeing you again. She's talked about nothing else for days.'

'Hasn't she?' Megan caught her lower lip between her teeth. 'Well, I'm looking forward to seeing her, too.' She moistened her lips. 'Um—how—how is your grandfather?' There, she'd said it. 'I suppose he must be ready to retire if he hasn't done so already.'

Was it her imagination or did Remy consider his words

before replying? 'Oh—Pops is still around,' he said vaguely, but it was obvious he didn't want to speak about him. Why? she wondered. Because he wasn't part of this package? Oh, God, she wasn't strong enough to handle Ryan's recriminations right now.

There was silence for a while, and Megan stared at the road passing under the car's wheels without really seeing it at all. She was hot, and even in the air-conditioned comfort of the car she felt uncomfortable. And she was nervous. Why had she agreed to put herself through this? she wondered. She had the feeling she was going to regret it, after all.

The speeding tarmac made her feel dizzy, and she cast a surreptitious look at her companion as he concentrated on the road. His profile was strong, despite the softening effect of thick dark lashes, and the moist hair that curled a little at his nape.

He was attractive, she thought wryly, aware that it was a long time since she had been affected by any man. Not that she was attracted to him, she told herself, except in a purely objective way. He was her 'nephew', after all. All he did was make her feel old.

'What's wrong?'

He was perceptive, too, and Megan hoped all her thoughts were not as obvious to him. She was going to have to get used to being around him without showing her feelings.

'Um—nothing,' she said, forcing a lighter tone. 'It's just—strange, being here again. It's quite a relief to see the island has hardly changed at all.'

Remy's straight brows ascended. 'Unlike me, you mean?' he queried, and she nodded.

'Well, of course.' She shrugged. 'We've all changed. I've only to look at you to see how much.'

'Don't patronise me, Megan—'

'I wasn't—'

'It sounded like it to me.' Remy's tawny eyes had darkened now, and she experienced an involuntary shiver. 'I guess it is hard for you to accept that we can meet on equal terms these days. You were always so conscious of your couple of years' superiority when we were young.'

Megan gasped. 'You make me sound like a prig.'

Remy's lips twitched. 'Do I?'

'And it wasn't—isn't—just couple of years' *seniority*—' she emphasised the word '—between us.' She moistened her lips. 'You were just five or six, the last time I saw you. I was nearly fifteen!' She grimaced. 'A teenager, no less.'

'I was nearly nine,' declared Remy doggedly. 'I'm twenty-five, Megan, so don't act like I'm just out of school.'

Megan swallowed. 'I didn't mean to offend you...'

'You haven't.' Remy's lips twisted. 'But stop making such a big thing about your age.' He slowed at the intersection before taking the turning towards El Serrat instead of the island's capital. 'Still—as you're practically senile, haven't you ever felt the urge to get married?'

Megan felt a nervous laugh bubble up into her throat, but at least it was better than sparring with him. 'Not lately,' she confessed. 'I've been too busy. Being your own boss can be a pain as well as a pleasure.'

'Yeah, I know.'

His response was too laconic, and she gave him a curious look. 'You know?'

'Sure.' His thigh flexed as he changed gear. 'I work for myself, too. I guess it's not so high-powered, but it pays the rent.'

Megan looked at him. 'I suppose you run the hotel now?'

'Hell, no.' He shook his head. 'I guess you could say I have more sense than to work for Mom. No,' he said again, 'I'm a lawyer. I've got a small practice in Port Serrat.'

'A lawyer!' Megan couldn't help the incredulity in her tone.

'Yeah, a lawyer,' he repeated. 'A grown-up one as well. I actually defend naughty people in court.'

Megan could feel the colour seeping into her throat. 'There's no need to be sarcastic.'

'Then quit acting like my maiden aunt.'

'Well—that's what I am,' said Megan, with a rueful smile. Then, 'All right. I apologise. I guess I've got a lot to learn about—about all of you. So—how's your mother? She does still work in the hotel?'

Remy expelled a resigned breath, as if her words had hardly pacified him at all. Then, 'Yeah,' he said. 'She practically runs the place these days.'

'And she's never married?' asked Megan, hoping to keep their conversation on a less—personal level, but the look Remy levelled at her was hardly sympathetic.

'To make me legitimate, you mean?' he asked, and she wanted to kick herself. 'No, I guess you could say Pops is the only father-figure I've ever known.'

'That wasn't what I meant, and you know it,' said Megan defensively. 'Only she's still a—a comparatively young woman. I thought she might have—fallen in love.'

'Perhaps she loved my father,' said Remy sardonically. 'However unlikely that might seem. Besides—' his lips adopted a cruel line '—I wouldn't have thought love meant that much to you.'

Megan's jaw sagged. 'I beg your—'

'Well, you did abandon the woman who loved you for a man without any perceptible emotions that I could see,' he continued, with some heat. 'Your mother loved you, Megan. Or have you conveniently forgotten that? How can you talk about love when you broke her heart?'

CHAPTER TWO

Now why had he said that?

Remy's hands clenched on the wheel, and he couldn't bear to look her in the face. It wasn't as if what had happened was anything to do with him, after all. He had no right to criticise her when she'd been too young to understand what was going on either.

She seemed to be speechless, and he was uneasily aware that the colour had now drained from her cheeks. For a moment there he'd forgotten how seriously ill she had been, and he felt as guilty as hell for upsetting her this way.

'Look—I'm sorry,' he began harshly, wishing they were still on the wide airport road where he might have been able to stop and apologise properly, instead of on the narrow road to El Serrat. He dared not stop here, not on one of these bends, where he'd be taking their lives into his hands. He'd done enough without risking an accident as well.

'My—my father loved me,' she said, almost as if she hadn't heard him. 'He loved me, and he'd done nothing wrong. How do you think he felt when he found out my mother had been cheating on him with your grandfather? My God! He'd made a friend of the man! How would you feel if it happened to you?'

Remy's mouth compressed. 'Like I said—'

'You're sorry?' Megan appeared to be trembling now, and he hoped he hadn't ruined everything by speaking his mind. 'Well, I'm sorry, but that's not good enough. And if your mother feels the same way I suggest you turn around and take me back to the airport.'

'She doesn't.' Remy swore. 'Ah, hell, she'd be furious with me if she knew what I'd said. Okay, you have your memories of what happened, and I accept that. But I lived with your mother for almost six years. Believe me, she was devastated when you wouldn't come to see her. You were the only child she had.'

Megan slanted a cool look in his direction. She looked like the Megan he remembered, even if the plump, pretty features she'd had as a child were now refined into a pale beauty, but she wasn't the same. The softness had gone, replaced by a brittle defensiveness, and he wondered if he had been naïve in thinking he might be able to change her mind.

'Was I?' she asked pointedly, and he had to concentrate for a moment to remember what he'd said.

He blew out a breath. 'You're talking about the miscarriage,' he intimated at last. 'She was devastated when she lost the baby. And it didn't help when your father wrote and told her she deserved it, too.'

Megan gasped. 'He didn't do that.'

'No.' Remy conceded the point. 'His actual words were, "God moves in mysterious ways." He didn't say that he was sorry for what had happened. That he understood how she must be feeling or anything like that.'

'He was hurt—'

'So was she.'

Megan's hands were clenched together in her lap, he noticed, but her voice was dispassionate as she spoke. 'Well, I don't know why she bothered to let Daddy know what had happened. It wasn't as if—as if it mattered to him.'

'Perhaps she hoped for some words of comfort,' said Remy flatly. 'Your father was supposed to be a man of God, after all.'

'He was also human,' retorted Megan tightly. 'Would she have expected him to congratulate her if the baby had lived?'

Remy silenced the angry retort that rose inside him. It wasn't fair to blame her for her father's sins. And who knew what he might have done if he'd been in the same position? It was easy to see both sides when you weren't involved.

'I believe your work is in the fashion industry,' he forced himself to say at last, in an attempt to change the subject. 'Mom said something about a catalogue. Do you sell mail-order or what?'

'Do you really want to know?'

Megan was terse, and he couldn't altogether blame her. His mother was hoping to heal old wounds, but all he'd done was exacerbate them.

'Look,' he said, feeling obliged to try and mend fences before they got to the hotel, 'forget what I said, okay? What do I know anyway? Like you said, I was only a kid. Kids see things in black and white. I guess you did, too.'

Megan glanced at him again, her eyes shadowed beneath lowered lids. She had beautiful eyes, he noticed; they shaded from indigo to violet within the feathery curl of her lashes, and glinted as if with unshed tears. He knew a totally unexpected urge to rub his thumb across her lids, to feel their salty moisture against his skin. Her face was porcelain-smooth, and so pale he could see the veins in her temple, see the pulse beating under the skin. He knew a sudden urge to skim his tongue over that pulse, to feel its rhythmic fluttering against his lips. To taste it, to taste her— He fought back the thought. Megan hadn't come to San Felipe because of him.

He dragged his eyes back to the road, stunned by the sudden heat of his arousal. For God's sake, he thought, was he completely out of his mind? What the hell was he doing even thinking such things? This woman wouldn't touch him with a bosun's hook.

'You didn't want me to come here, did you, Remy?'

Her question, coming totally out of the blue, startled him. In his present state of mind, that was the last thing he'd have said. But then, she didn't know how he was feeling, thank God! She couldn't feel the tight constriction of his jeans.

'That's not true,' he got out at last, feeling his palms

sliding sweatily on the wheel. It irritated him beyond belief that he'd betrayed any bias to her, but it irritated him still more that he couldn't control himself.

'So why are you giving me such a hard time?' she asked, and he was aware of her watching him with a wary gaze.

'I'm not,' he said tensely, giving in to his frustration. 'I just don't think you're entirely even-handed when it comes to your parents. Your father was a vindictive bastard.' He paused. 'I should know.'

Megan had been given the penthouse suite, which, in island terms, meant that her rooms were on the sixth floor of the hotel. None of the hotels that had sprung up along the coast was allowed to build beyond six floors and these days, she had noticed, there were quite a number of new ones.

Which meant, Megan assumed somewhat uneasily, that the Robards were sacrificing quite a large slice of their income by accommodating her in such luxurious surroundings. This was, after all, their most lucrative time of year, when the island was flooded with visitors from North America and Northern Europe escaping the cold weather back home.

Yet, despite her anxieties—and the fact that by the time they'd reached the hotel she and Remy had barely been on speaking terms—Anita had made her feel welcome. The other woman had behaved as if it were sixteen weeks—not sixteen years—since she had last come here. She had greeted her stepsister with affection, and dispelled the apprehension Remy had aroused.

Anita had been waiting on the verandah of the hotel when the estate car had swept down the drive. Megan had barely had time to admire the hedges of scarlet hibiscus that hid the building from the road before her stepsister was jerking the door open and pulling Megan out into her arms. There had been tears then, tears that Megan couldn't hide even from Remy. She was still so weak, she'd defended herself silently. Any kind of emotion just broke her up.

Blinking rapidly, she'd been grateful for the cooling

breeze that swept in off the ocean. Apart from the immediate area surrounding the hotel, where artificially watered lawns and palm trees provided the guests with oases of greenness, the milk-white sands stretched as far as the eye could see. But she hadn't been able to ignore the fact of the car door opening behind her, or Remy getting out and walking around to the back of the vehicle to unload her bags.

'Oh, Megan,' Anita was saying as she hugged her in her protective embrace, 'it's been far too long. It's a sad thing if you have to be at death's door before you'll accept our invitation.'

Our invitation?

Megan wondered who Anita included in that statement. Not Remy, surely. But she could only shake her head, unaccountably moved by her stepsister's welcome. After the way Remy had behaved, she'd been dreading this moment.

And Anita had hardly changed at all. She'd been pleasantly plump as a teenager, and she was plump still, with round dimpled features that could never disguise her feelings to anyone. As before, she was wearing one of the loose-fitting tee shirts and the baggy shorts she had always favoured, her curly dark hair scooped up in a ponytail.

Yet, despite her welcome, Megan sensed that Anita wasn't quite as carefree as she'd like her to think. She noticed as the other woman drew back that there were dark lines around her eyes, and a trace of more than wistfulness in her tears.

But perhaps she was being over-sensitive, Megan considered, and, avoiding Remy's eyes, she allowed Anita to lead her into the hotel. She found some relief in admiring the changes that had been made and consoled herself with the thought that this was the most difficult time for all of them. No matter how accommodating they might try to be, they couldn't ignore the past.

A fountain now formed a centre-piece in the newly designed foyer, with the lounges and reception area moved to the floor above. 'I suggest I show you your room and let you freshen up before dinner,' Anita declared, leading the way across to the bank of lifts. 'I imagine you could do with a rest. Did you have a pleasant journey?'

The lifts were new, too, much different from the grilled cage that Megan remembered. Would her mother have become so enamoured with the place if it had always been as impersonal as this? she wondered. Laura had always said it was the informality of Robards Reach that made it so unique...

'There's so much I want to tell you,' Anita continued as they went up in the lift—not with Remy and the luggage, Megan was relieved to find. 'So much time we have to make up. I want to know all about what's been happening in your life. Your boyfriend—partner—' She coloured. 'Simon, isn't it? He sounds really nice. I'm glad you've found a decent man to care for you.'

'He doesn't—that is—' Megan pressed her lips together and didn't go on. As with Remy, she was loath to deny that she and Simon were an item. She didn't know when it might be useful to have that excuse to turn to, and, hoping Anita would put the colour in her face down to the heat, she finished, 'It was good of you to—to invite me here.'

'Well, it's not as if it was the first time,' declared Anita, with a trace of censure, but with none of the aggression her son had shown. 'Anyway, it's so good to see you.' She took a breath. 'You're so like—so like Laura when I first knew her.' She touched Megan's face. 'It's going to be hard for—for my father.' Her lips tightened. 'But you're so pale. We'll have to try and put some colour into those cheeks before you leave.'

Anita left her alone in the luxurious suite then, ostensibly to allow her to relax for a while before dinner. Megan was grateful for the respite, grateful that she was going to have a breathing space before meeting Ryan Robards, but she doubted she'd relax in her present mood.

A bellboy brought her luggage. When the polite tap sounded at her door, she was apprehensive for a moment, expecting Remy to bring her suitcases in. But she should have known better. As he had told her, he was a lawyer, not a hotel employee.

Although she was tempted to step out onto the balcony, where a cushioned lounger and several wicker chairs were set beneath a bougainvillaea-hung awning, Megan decided that a shower might liven her up. It would be too easy to get disheartened, particularly as her body clock was still on European time, and she determined to concentrate on the positive aspects of her trip. Who wouldn't like to recuperate in such surroundings? She had four whole weeks to get completely well.

Which was part of the problem, she acknowledged, when she stepped into the mosaic-tiled shower and turned on the gold-plated taps. At this point in time, four weeks seemed like a lifetime. She'd never have committed herself to such a long stay if it had been left to her.

But it hadn't been left to her. Simon had made all the arrangements while she was still too weak to protest. It was too long since she'd taken a real holiday, he'd told her. She needed plenty of time to recover her strength.

By the time she went downstairs again, Megan was feeling considerably better.

When she'd emerged from the bathroom, wrapped in one of the soft towelling robes the hotel provided, it was to find a tray of tea and biscuits awaiting her. While she'd been taking her shower, someone—Anita, she guessed—had let herself into the suite and deposited the tray on the round table by the window. There was milk and cream, and several kinds of home-made biscuits. Although she'd been sure she wasn't hungry, she'd sampled all the biscuits, and drunk three cups of tea as well.

Afterwards, she'd rested on the square colonial bed that was set on a dais, so that its occupants could see the sea. Megan had watched the darkening waters of the Caribbean until the sun had disappeared into the ocean, and then she guessed she'd dozed for perhaps another hour after that.

She'd awakened to a darkened room and for a few moments she'd felt a sense of disorientation. But then she'd switched on the lamps, and the memory of her arrival had come back to her. She hadn't felt much like resting after that.

Still, after unpacking her suitcases, there'd been plenty of time to get ready for dinner. Anita had told her to come down at eight, but not to worry if she was late. There were often problems associated with the hotel that required her attention, and if she wasn't there Megan should just make herself at home.

As if she could do that! Going down in the lift, Megan had to admit that such an instruction was probably beyond her. Besides, what if Ryan Robards was waiting for her? What on earth was she going to say to him?

The apartments the family used were on the first floor, immediately behind the reception area. Megan was familiar with them, of course. Before the ugly break-up of her parents' marriage, the Crosses and their daughter had often had drinks with Ryan Robards and Anita. In those days, Megan and her parents had rented one of the cottages that stood in the grounds and belonged to the hotel. Her father had always preferred self-catering to the blandness of hotel food, but because of his love for sailing he and Ryan had become good friends...

Now, Megan stepped out of the lift feeling decidedly self-conscious. It was some time since she had taken as much trouble with her appearance, but for some reason she had felt the need to make an effort tonight. But although the black silk leggings and matching beaded top were perfectly presentable she was intensely aware that they exposed the narrow contours of her bones.

A belief that was made even more apparent when she entered her stepsister's sitting room to find only Remy waiting for her. He was standing at the open French doors that led out onto a private terrace, one hand supporting himself against the screen, the other wrapped around a glass.

The indrawn breath she took upon seeing him attracted his attention, and he swung round at once, surveying her with cool shaded eyes. What was he thinking? she wondered as his brows arched in a silent acknowledgement of her presence. After what he had said earlier, she wasn't sure what to expect.

His appraisal of her appearance was deliberate, she thought. Was he trying to intimidate her, or was he simply waiting to see what her reaction would be? He was far too sure of himself, she thought, stiffening her resolve not to let any of them upset her. Yet, as she felt her features hardening, his unaccountably softened.

'Feeling better?' he enquired, before swallowing the remainder of the liquid in his glass with one gulp. 'Let me get you a drink. You can probably use one.'

Could she not?

Megan linked her hands together at her waist and contemplated the advantages that alcohol could bring. It would certainly make this interview easier, smooth the rough edges of her tension, so to speak. But her doctor had been quite specific, and she had no desire to fall ill again.

'Um—do you have a mineral water?' she asked at last, and he regarded her with narrowed eyes.

'A mineral water?'

'I'm still on medication,' she explained, moving further into the room, even though she would have preferred to keep her distance from him. She swallowed. 'Where's your mother? She asked me to join her here.'

'She won't be long,' replied Remy, depositing his empty glass on the small bar that was recessed into the wall. He examined the row of small bottles that occupied one shelf in the refrigerated cabinet. 'Mineral water, you said,' he murmured thoughtfully. 'Yeah, here we are. Will sparkling water do?'

'Fine,' said Megan quickly, moving across the room and taking up his former position by the French doors. Beyond the terrace, the sound of the sea was a muted thunder, the warmth of the night air scented with spice and pine.

'There you go.'

He was behind her suddenly, his reflection visible in the

glass door, his height and darkness disturbingly close. Once
again, she was made aware of how the years had changed
him. It was difficult to remember now exactly what she had
expected.

'Oh—thanks,' she said, half turning towards him to take
the glass, her efforts to avoid brushing his lean, tanned
fingers almost causing an accident. Only a swift recovery
on his part prevented the glass from ending up on the floor,
and a splash of ice-cold liquid stung her leg.

'Dammit!' Remy stared down impatiently at the damp
spot on her leggings, and Megan felt like a fool. 'What the
hell did you do that for?' he demanded. 'I'm not contami-
nated, you know.'

'I didn't do it on purpose!' she exclaimed, even though
she doubted he believed her. 'I—I wasn't thinking. You
startled me, that's all.' She brushed her leg almost dismiss-
ively. 'Anyway, there's no harm done.'

'Isn't there?'

She wasn't sure what he was referring to, so she chose
to say nothing, relieved when he walked back to the bar.
But he was back a few moments later, holding a napkin,
and, squatting down on his haunches in front of her, he
pressed the white linen against her leg.

'Oh—please.' He was really embarrassing her now, and
she attempted to take the napkin from him. 'Let me,' she
said. 'Let me do that.' But he merely tipped his head back
and cast her an ironic look and carried on.

She glanced down, her eyes unwillingly drawn to his
bent head. His hair was glistening with moisture, she noticed, tiny drops of water shining on the dark strands. He
had either taken a shower or a swim while she'd been resting, she reflected, the images her thoughts were evoking
causing a moistness in her palms.

She sighed. Why couldn't she ignore him? Yet, crouched
in front of her as he was, she would have had to be numb
as well as blind not to notice the straining seam between
his legs. Despite her irritation with him earlier, she couldn't

deny his sexuality. It was as natural to him as breathing. Just like his grandfather's had been...

'Will—will Mr Robards be joining us?' she asked stiffly—anything to distract herself from what he was doing—and as if her words had diverted him, too, he rose abruptly to his feet.

'I guess I owe you an apology, don't I?' he said, without answering her question. 'I was an ignorant lout before. I'm sorry.'

Megan was confused. 'Oh—well, I—it was my fault really—'

'I don't mean for spilling your drink,' he contradicted her drily. 'I mean for the way I spoke to you in the car. I guess I had no right to criticise you or your father as I did.'

'Oh.' Megan let her breath out slowly. She was finding it difficult to keep abreast of his changes of mood. Or at least that was the excuse she gave herself. But there was no denying that he disturbed her, and it would be fatally easy to respond to his charm. 'Let's forget it, shall we?'

'I'm forgiven?'

'Of course.' She was abrupt.

'Is your drink all right?'

Her glass was still more than half full, and she hurriedly took a sip. 'It's delicious,' she said, hoping she sounded more controlled than she felt. 'Um—will your grandfather be joining us?'

Remy hesitated for a moment, and then he shook his head. 'Not tonight,' he said, his tone flatter now. 'And I've got to be getting back to town myself.'

'You don't live here?'

Megan realised at once that her response had been far too revealing. Dammit, she should have guessed he'd have his own place as soon as he'd told her he worked in Port Serrat.

'I have an apartment near the harbour,' he said, his eyes assessing her. 'It's handy for the office. Like tonight, I sometimes have to work in the evenings.'

She swallowed. 'You're working this evening?' she asked, managing to sound less daunted, and he smiled.

'I've a client who works in one of the hotels,' he explained. 'It's difficult for him to keep sociable hours.'

'So you accommodate him?'

'I'm an accommodating fellow,' he remarked mockingly, and she realised how easily he could disconcert her. How did he do that, when she was usually so at ease with men? It was as if he had a conduit to her soul.

'So,' she persevered firmly, 'do you often work long hours?'

'When I have to.' He shrugged. 'Otherwise I'd like nothing better than to join you and Mom for dinner.' His eyes held hers with deliberate provocation. 'I can't wait to hear what you've been doing with yourself. Apart from nearly killing yourself, that is.'

Megan shook her head. 'It was hardly that.'

'I heard it was,' he contradicted her gently. 'Is that why you're so edgy? Or is it just me?'

Megan coloured then. She couldn't help it. She could feel the heat spreading up her neck, darkening the exposed hollow of her throat, and seeping into her hairline.

'I'm not edgy,' she denied, producing a smile that probably gave her words the lie. 'I'm tired, I suppose, but that's understandable. It's been a long day.'

'Yeah, I guess it has,' he said, his tone softening. He lifted one hand and to her dismay he rubbed his knuckles along the curve of her jawline. 'You'll feel better in the morning. All you need is a good night's sleep.'

Megan drew her chin back automatically. His warm knuckles were absurdly sensual, hinting at an intimacy she couldn't begin to cope with.

She didn't say anything, but she knew he was aware of her withdrawal. His hand fell to his side, and his eyes narrowed on the way her chest rose and fell in a nervous display.

'Relax,' he said. 'What are you afraid of? I'm not going to hurt you.'

'I never—I don't know what you mean—'

Megan stumbled to deny his mocking accusation, but before she could get coherency into her words Anita's voice interrupted them.

'I'm sorry, Megan—' she was saying as she came into the room, before breaking off in some surprise when she saw her son. 'Why, Remy!' she exclaimed, not without some asperity. 'I thought you were leaving half an hour ago.'

There was an awkward pause, when Megan wondered if what had gone before was visible on their faces, and then Remy seemed to find his voice. 'Well, as you can see, I'm still here,' he remarked tersely. 'I wasn't aware I had to report my whereabouts to you.'

Anita flushed, as stung by his words in her turn as Megan had been earlier. 'You don't, of course,' she said. 'But I could have done with your assistance. The air-conditioning went out in one of the bungalows, and I couldn't get in touch with Carlos.'

'Have you fixed it?'

Remy was slightly less aggressive now, and his mother took a steadying breath. 'At last,' she said. 'It was only a fuse, thank goodness. But—but—your grandfather's rather fractious this evening, and I didn't really have the time to go charging about looking for spares.'

'I'm sorry.'

There was still an edge to Remy's voice, and, realising she should say something in his defence, Megan chipped in. 'Um—Remy's been keeping me company, I'm afraid,' she said apologetically. 'I probably delayed him, or he would have been gone.'

Anita managed a faint smile. 'Don't give it another thought. Either of you,' she added, looking at her son. 'I'm sorry if I sounded harassed. It's just one of the joys of running a hotel.'

Remy straightened his spine. 'Then I guess I will get going.' He looked at Megan. 'Now that you've got my mother to entertain you, you won't need me any more. Enjoy your evening, won't you? I'll think of you while I'm earning my lonely crust.'

'Oh, don't be silly, Remy.' Anita evidently thought her son's manner was due to what she'd said, but Megan wasn't so sure. 'Naturally, if I'd thought you had the time to stay and have a drink with us, I'd have suggested it. It was you who said you had work to do this evening.'

'And I do,' said Remy flatly, arching a mocking brow in Megan's direction. 'I'll see you—both—later, though maybe not tomorrow. I've got to go to the Beaufort plantation in the afternoon.'

'All right, darling.' Reassured, Anita gave her son's arm a squeeze. 'Give my love to Rachel when you see her, won't you? Tell her it's been far too long since she's come to visit.'

CHAPTER THREE

MEGAN slept fitfully, even though she was tired, waking the next morning before it was really light. Even the lingering effects of her illness were not enough to counter her body's rhythms. It was obvious her system was still running on London time.

She lay for a little while mulling over the events of the previous evening. She knew now that Anita's invitation had not been as spontaneous as it had at first appeared. Oh, her stepsister was pleased to see her, and she had been concerned when she'd learned Megan had had an operation. But she had had another reason altogether for making the call that had brought her stepsister to San Felipe.

Not that Megan had learned that immediately.

After Remy's departure, they had both felt the need to get their relationship back on an even footing, and while Anita had a martini, and during the course of their dinner—which was taken on the candlelit terrace—they had talked about less personal things.

Then, at Anita's instigation, Megan had told her how she had come to be in the hospital. Her stepsister had seemed to find it incredible that Megan should have developed an ulcer at her age. She didn't seem to understand the stresses and strains involved in trying to start a business, and Megan had been loath to tell her that the specialist had intimated that she might have had the ulcer since she was in her teens.

'And are your rooms comfortable?' Anita asked at last, clearly eager that Megan should have every opportunity to relax while she was here.

'They're perfect,' Megan assured her. 'I just don't think I should be taking up such luxurious apartments. This must be the busiest time of the year for you.'

'You're family. Where else would I put you?' Anita re-torted firmly. 'And it's not as if you haven't always been welcome. I told you when—when your mother died that you had an open invitation. Any time you'd wanted to come for a visit, you had only to pick up the phone.'

Right. Megan nodded politely, wondering somewhat cynically how often she had said those same words herself. In business, people often offered hospitality without mean-ing it. And contacting the Robards had never been on her list of priorities.

'Anyway,' went on Anita, as if sensing the other woman's reservations, 'you're here now, and that's what matters.' She gave a rueful smile. 'I bet you were surprised to see Remy at the airport. He told me that you thought he was some toy-boy trying to pick you up.'

Hardly that, thought Megan indignantly, feeling some-what hurt that Anita should feel the need to tell her exactly what Remy had said. Besides, it was not what he had said to her, though perhaps his assertion that they could meet on equal terms had been meant to flatter her, after all.

'I didn't recognise him,' she admitted, and Anita gave a short laugh.

'I don't suppose you did,' she said. 'He was just a boy the last time you saw him. Did he tell you he got a law degree? He's started his own practice in town.'

'Yes.' But Megan was aware that her stepsister's expla-nation had caused a sudden tightening in her stomach. It was Anita's persistence in treating Megan like an equal that disturbed her. Which was silly after the way she'd reacted to what Remy had said.

'We're very proud of him,' went on Anita, clearly taking Megan's silence as a cue to elaborate. 'Even his grandfather sings his praises, when he isn't grumbling about him ne-glecting the hotel. I think we were all afraid when he went to college in the States that he wouldn't come back.'

'But he did.'

Anita nodded. 'Despite—well, despite everything, this is still his home. I don't think he'd be happy living in Boston or New York, even though he could have earned a lot more money there.'

'I'm sure.'

Megan was impressed in spite of herself, understanding a little of Anita's pride in her son. After all, he was her only child. And because she'd never got married their relationship was that much more special.

'Of course, Rachel probably had something to do with it,' added Anita, pulling a wry face, and Megan was reminded of her stepsister's remark when Remy was leaving. She'd said, 'Give my love to Rachel,' but Megan hadn't paid much attention to it then. She'd been too relieved that Remy was leaving after the tenseness of their exchange, and she supposed she'd assumed the woman worked for him or something.

'Rachel?' she said now, faintly, hoping her tone didn't imply anything more than a casual interest, and Anita nodded.

'Rachel De Vries,' she said comfortably. 'Her family own the De Vries plantation that adjoins the land we own on the other side of the island. Her father sits in the local legislature. Remy and Rachel have been dating one another since they were in their teens.'

'I see.'

Megan was impatient at the feeling of emptiness this news engendered. For heaven's sake, she thought, what did it matter to her? Despite what Simon had said she intended to stay here as short a time as possible. She'd find some excuse for leaving, and then their lives would go on as before.

'Of course, I live in hope,' continued Anita ruefully, and Megan forced herself to respond.

'In hope of what?'

'Of him getting married, naturally!' exclaimed Anita, reaching across the table to tap Megan's hand. 'I want to be a grandmother, before I'm too old for it to be any fun.'

Megan sought refuge in her wine glass at that point. Despite her medication, she'd decided that one glass of wine wouldn't hurt her, and she was grateful now for the diversion it offered. For all the room was air-conditioned, she was feeling uncomfortably hot suddenly. This was harder than she'd expected, and she hadn't even met Ryan Robards yet.

'Anyway, I'm sure you must be tired of me going on about Remy,' Anita concluded, possibly putting Megan's restlessness down to the fact that she was bored. She shook her head. 'Tell me about your job. What is it you do exactly?'

'Oh—I'm sure you're not really interested in my work,' said Megan hurriedly. 'I believe Simon told you about the directory, and that's all it is. My role is fairly simple; I'm just the gofer. I coordinate the designs, and deal with the printers and so on.'

'I'm sure it's not as simple as all that,' declared Anita reprovingly, but, as if sensing that Megan didn't really want to elaborate, she chose another topic. 'I know your—father would have been very proud of you. You always were the apple of his eye.'

'Perhaps.'

Megan wasn't at all sure that Giles Cross would have approved of his daughter getting involved in a business that was so trivial—in his eyes, at least. He'd expected so much of her. Without her mother to mediate, it hadn't been easy.

'Well, whatever.' Anita's lips tightened. 'It's not as if he could have expected you to follow in his footsteps.'

'No.'

'There are so few women in the ministry—none at all here—and his work was very demanding.' Anita frowned. 'He put so much of himself into his work. Your mother said you were often on your own.'

Megan caught her breath. 'We didn't mind.'

'*You* didn't.'

'Are you saying that my mother did?'

Anita sighed. 'Laura was a wonderful, vital woman, Megan. Of course she minded.' She paused. 'Particularly as your father didn't have to do as much as he did. All ●

those missions to African countries, for example. Why didn't he ever take your mother along?'

Megan stiffened her back. 'She didn't want to go.'

'That's not true. To begin with, she'd have gone anywhere with him to try and make their marriage work. The trouble was, he wouldn't let her leave the parish. You must know your father preferred to travel alone.'

Megan swallowed. 'What are you implying?'

'I'm not implying anything, Megan. I'm telling you that your mother was not wholly to blame for what happened. If it hadn't been my father it would have been someone else, can't you see that? She needed company; companionship; love.'

'She seemed happy enough until she came here.'

Anita gave a wry smile. 'Oh, Megan, you're a woman now. Can't you understand what I'm trying to tell you? Your mother wasn't—wasn't the evil woman your father tried to make her. She was just lonely, that's all.'

'And your father took advantage of that!' exclaimed Megan bitterly. 'Oh, Anita, we're never going to agree on this. Can we just—change the subject, please?'

'If you insist.' But Anita looked a little disappointed now, and Megan wished she'd been a little more forthcoming about her work. At least that was a safe subject, despite what she thought about her relationship with Simon.

'Anyway,' Megan continued, 'Remy said you practically run the hotel single-handed these days. I think he said your father had retired.'

'Oh, God!' Anita took a deep breath, and then, as if she couldn't sit still any longer, she got to her feet and paced about the room. 'If only that was true.'

'What do you mean?'

Megan was confused now, and Anita turned to give her a strangely bitter look. 'You don't know, do you? Remy never told you? Well, of course, he couldn't. He doesn't know the truth himself.'

'Told me what?'

'That his grandfather's very ill?'

Megan shook her head. 'No.' She moistened her lips. 'I—I'm sorry to hear that.'

'Are you?' Anita's tone hadn't altered, and Megan wondered why she was looking at her with such a wealth of emotion burning behind her eyes. 'Yes. Maybe you mean it. For his sake, I hope you do.'

'Anita!' Megan's hands gripped the arms of her chair. 'What is it? What's the matter? Why are you looking at me like that?'

'He's dying, Megan,' replied the other woman tremulously. 'That's why I rang you, why I begged you to come. I've been carrying the burden alone for so long, and I—I need someone to talk to, to share the pain.'

'But Remy—'

'I've told you, he knows his grandfather is ill, but that's all. I—I couldn't tell him the truth. He and his grandfather are so close. He's going to be devastated when he finds out.'

'Oh, Anita!' Megan got up from her chair then, and almost without thinking how her stepsister might react she went to her and put her arms around her. 'Anita,' she said again as the older woman clutched at her with desperate fingers. 'I'm so sorry. If there's anything I can do, you only have to ask.'

It was little wonder she had slept fitfully, thought Megan now, throwing back the sheet and sliding her legs out of bed. Such sleep as she had had had been punctuated by dreams of her father and mother, and her own encounters with Remy, who apparently was unaware of how ill his grandfather really was.

Biting her lower lip, Megan crossed the floor to the windows and, unlatching them, stepped out onto the balcony. Even at this hour of the morning the temperature was warm, and a little sultry, too, the clouds hanging over the horizon a lingering reminder of the rain that had come in the night. Megan had heard it pattering against the panes, and it had reminded her of how she and Remy used to go hunting for crabs after a storm when they were children. The pools that had dotted the shoreline had been a source of all sorts of exciting mysteries, with seashells and other flotsam capturing their attention.

Propping her elbows on the wrought-iron rail, Megan gazed out now at a view that was still disturbingly familiar. Beyond the paved walks and exotically planted gardens of the hotel, white coral sand edged an ocean that was fringed with foam. Seabirds swooped along the beach, always scavenging, and in the distance the tide turned to mist against the rocks. It was all inexpressibly beautiful—a tropical paradise that was no less magical than she remembered.

Or was it?

Certainly, her father would have said it had its serpent. The wonderful holiday island he had found had turned into a nightmare for him. She knew he would not have approved of her coming here, consorting with the enemy. Even if Ryan Robards was a very sick man. That didn't excuse his behaviour of years before.

Yet she couldn't deny feeling a certain compassion for the man. She was not a vindictive creature by nature, and although she would not have chosen to see her mother's husband again she did have sympathy for him. And, after all, before her parents had separated, she had regarded Remy's grandfather as a kind of surrogate uncle. He had been kind to her in those days. Had his affection only been a means to get close to her mother, as her father had said?

Whatever, in the beginning, Megan had looked forward to their holidays in San Felipe with great excitement. She remembered the girls at the exclusive day school she had attended had all envied her those yearly trips to El Serrat. She hadn't even been too upset when her father hadn't always been able to accompany them, though later on she'd realised that that was when her mother's affair with Ryan Robards had begun.

She'd been eight years old when she'd first come to the island, and almost fifteen when her parents had divorced. She had no idea how long her mother and Ryan Robards had been conducting their relationship; she only knew that her father had been the one who had been badly hurt.

What had always amazed her was how her mother could have allowed herself to become involved with someone like Ryan in the first place. All right, he was fun to be with, but compared to her father he was brash and insensitive, and lacking in any formal education. Indeed, in the early days of their relationship, Megan could remember her father laughing about some expression Ryan had used in error. He'd described the other man as a philistine, although Megan hadn't understood then what he had meant.

Looking back, she conceded that there must have been more to what had happened than she'd imagined. No one gave up almost twenty years of marriage on a whim. She'd been far too defensive of her father to listen to any explanation her mother might have given her. She'd been totally prejudiced, she acknowledged, not prepared to give her mother a chance.

After the divorce, Megan had never gone back to San Felipe. She'd seen her mother from time to time, but always at some neutral location. Then, six years after Laura had married Ryan, she had developed an obscure form of cancer that was incurable. Although she'd been treated in a London hospital, and Megan had spent a lot of time with her, the looming presence of her new husband had prevented any real reconciliation being made.

Not that Megan had seen Ryan then, nor afterwards at her mother's funeral service. She had been too distressed herself, too concerned about her father, who had taken his ex-wife's death very badly, to pay any attention to either Ryan or Anita. Afterwards, after the cremation, she'd learned that Ryan had taken his wife's remains back to San Felipe to be scattered in a garden of remembrance there. It had been the final bereavement so far as Giles Cross was concerned—the realisation that there was nothing left of the woman he had loved.

His death some six months later, in what could only be described as suspicious circumstances, had left Megan completely alone. She had been in her final year at college, and to learn that her father had died from an overdose of the painkiller he'd been taking for some time, and with whose properties he was perfectly familiar, had been the final straw. She'd dropped out of college after his funeral, and rented a cottage on the Suffolk coast, spending several weeks in total isolation. She'd been trying to come to terms with her life, trying to understand how a man who had loved God, and to whom he had professed such allegiance, should have become so depressed that he'd taken his own life.

Eventually, loneliness—and the need to get a job—had driven her back to London. The vicarage, where she had lived for most of her young life, had now been occupied by another incumbent, and the few possessions left to her had had to be rescued from storage. What little money her father had left had been used to furnish a small, rented flat in Bayswater, and she'd initially got a job in an advertising agency to try and put some order back into her life.

It was soon after that that she'd run into Simon Chater again, and their eventual collaboration had led to her leaving the flat and sharing a house with him. It suited both of them to project a united image, and the fact that they both had their own rooms was no one's business but their own.

The sun had risen as she'd been musing, and, straightening, Megan stretched lazy arms above her head. There was no doubt she was feeling better this morning, but it was time to remove her scantily clad figure from public view.

She decided to have a shower and get dressed, and then take a pre-breakfast stroll along the shoreline. Anita was taking her to see Ryan at ten o'clock, but that gave her plenty of space. She refused to admit she was looking for a diversion. Good Lord, Ryan wasn't a monster, he was a very sick man.

By the time she had had her shower and dressed in cream silk shorts and a matching vest it was still barely seven o'clock. Slipping her feet into soft leather loafers, she surveyed her appearance critically. She didn't really want to wear make-up, but a touch of blusher and some lipstick seemed mandatory. She looked so pale otherwise, and she had no wish for her stepsister to suspect she hadn't slept.

The lift hummed silently to the ground floor, and when she stepped out into the marble foyer she was surprised to see that there were already guests about. Obviously, judging by their attire, they belonged to the indefatigable band of joggers who insisted on taking their exercise whatever the weather. For her part, Megan preferred to confine her activities to the gym.

Continental breakfast was being offered in the lobby in a small bar divided from the rest of the area by a vine-hung trellis, and, grateful to be anonymous for once, Megan helped herself to a warm Danish pastry and a cup of black coffee. Carrying them across to a small table, she settled herself by the window, deciding there were advantages to being here, after all.

She garnered a few interested glances from the men who passed her table, but for the most part she was left in peace. And it was pleasant sitting in the sunlight, with air-conditioning to mute the heat, munching on her apricot Danish and watching the world go by.

'I see you couldn't sleep.'

She hadn't seen him come into the lobby, if indeed he had just arrived at the hotel, and his lazy greeting caught her unawares. Child-like, she had torn the pastry apart and saved the apricot until last, and Remy discovered her savouring the juicy item, her lips moist and her fingers sticky from the fruit.

'Um—jet lag,' she mumbled, stuffing the rest of the apricot into her mouth and licking the tips of her fingers rather guiltily. 'Where did you come from anyway? I thought you said you lived in town.'

'I do.' Remy glanced behind him, then raising a hand, as if to impress her to stay where she was, he strode across to the buffet table and helped himself to a coffee. He was back almost before she had swallowed the remains of the apricot, swinging out the wicker chair opposite and straddling it, its back to the table. 'I thought I might join you for breakfast.'

Megan's eyes widened, but she tried not to let him see how his words had affected her. It was hard enough coming to terms with his appearance. In a beige silk shirt and the trousers of a navy suit, the jacket looped carelessly over one shoulder, he looked vastly different from the beachcomber she had met the day before. He looked—unfamiliar, she thought fancifully: dark, and enigmatic, and mature. And he was watching her with disturbing closeness, as if those tawny eyes could actually read her thoughts.

'I'm flattered,' she said, trying to keep her tone noncommittal. 'But how did you know I'd be up?'

'Jet lag?' he suggested, turning her words back on her before taking a mouthful of his coffee. And when her brows arched in disbelief he gave a grin. 'I hoped,' he added, with rather more diffidence. 'Of course, I didn't think I'd be lucky enough to find you here.'

Megan grimaced. 'Well, I admit, I never can adjust to the time change. I doubt I ever will.'

Remy folded his arms along the back of the chair and regarded her with a wry look. 'Any minute now you're going to tell me you're too old to change. Come off it, Megan, anyone knows a five-hour time lag takes some getting used to.'

Megan shrugged. 'If you say so.'

'I do say so.' He propped his chin on his wrist. 'Did you have a pleasant evening after I left?'

'Very pleasant, thank you.' Although that wasn't quite the description she would have used. 'Your mother and I are old friends. It was good to see her again.'

'I bet.' But Remy's expression was suddenly guarded. Then, as if overcoming some inner conflict, he said, 'I wished I could have stayed.'

'Yes.' But Megan didn't make the mistake of saying, So do I. She had no wish to rekindle those disturbing moments from the night before.

'Believe it or not, I enjoyed our conversation,' he continued evenly. 'I guess you're not what I expected, after all.'

'Why?' Megan was intrigued. 'I thought you said I'd hardly changed.'

'Physically, you haven't, but I've decided you're much nicer than you used to be. You were quite a little prig when you were younger.'

'I wasn't.'

'You were.' She suspected he was teasing her now, but she didn't quite know how to deal with him in this mood. 'You always thought you knew everything,' he insisted. 'I thought you were a smartarse, if you want the truth.'

Megan gasped. 'Well, thank you.'

He grinned. 'It's my pleasure.' He paused. 'Of course, as I said before, you've much improved. You're much more feminine for one thing. I'll never forget those khaki shorts you used to wear.'

Megan flushed. 'They weren't khaki. They were fawn. And all the church Scouts wore them.'

'Not the girl Scouts, I'll bet,' retorted Remy, laughing. 'Of course, you always wanted to be a boy.'

'I did not!'

Megan was defensive, but she couldn't deny that she had been a bossy creature in those days. It came from being an only child, she defended herself. And the suspicion that her father had wanted a son.

'Well, you weren't exactly a little angel,' she declared now. 'You practically frightened the life out of me when you put that frog in my bed.'

Remy chuckled reminiscently. 'It was only a little frog,' he protested, but Megan wouldn't have it.

'When it jumped out of the sheets, I nearly died.'

Remy grimaced. 'Well, thank goodness you didn't. I dread to think what your father would have said if he'd known. Which reminds me, I never did thank you for not telling him. And you were a lot nicer to me after that,' he added irrepressibly.

'I wonder why?' Megan pulled a face at him. 'I'd forgotten what a disgusting little boy you were.'

Remy's eyes darkened. 'Have I changed?' he asked with
sudden seriousness, and Megan coloured.

'I hope so,' she said, trying to keep the conversation
lighthearted, but Remy chose to put her on the spot.

'I mean it,' he said. 'Have I changed a lot? I'm interested
to hear what you think.'

Megan sighed, suddenly aware of the dangers of getting
too close to him. 'Of course you've changed,' she said hurriedly. 'You're sixteen years older to begin with.' She
paused. 'Your mother's very proud of you, you know.'

Remy regarded her through narrowed lids. 'Is she?' he
said carelessly. 'Well, that's some consolation, I suppose.
But it doesn't really answer my question.' He grimaced. 'I
doubt your father would have been so reticent about what
he thought.'

Megan doubted it, too. Although Giles Cross had made
time for Ryan Robards, he had had little patience with
Anita and her young son. In private, he'd expressed the
view that as soon as Anita had discovered she was pregnant
she should have arranged to have the baby adopted. He
would never have allowed his daughter to be a fifteen-year-
old mother.

Of course, Anita's circumstances had been different from
those of the girls in his parish in England. Megan remembered her mother making that argument very well. Although Ryan Robards had been born in the United States,
he and his wife had moved from Florida to the island of
San Felipe when Anita was little more than a baby. He'd
sold up his business in Miami and opened the hotel at El
Serrat.

In consequence, Anita had been brought up with the local
girls, many of whom were married by the time they were
fifteen years old. And perhaps she would have got married,
too, if her mother hadn't been killed in a plane crash when
Anita was just a schoolgirl. As it was, she'd stayed to take

care of her father and had always seemed an integral part of the hotel...

'Anyway,' Remy went on after a moment, 'despite everything, I was sorry to hear that Mr Cross had died. It was just after Laura's death, wasn't it? It must have been hard for you at that time.'

'It was.' Megan looked down at the dregs of coffee in her cup. 'It was daunting to feel completely on my own. My parents were only children, you see, and their parents were dead. For a time, I didn't know what I was going to do.'

'You could have come here,' pointed out Remy gently, and Megan realised it had been a real option for them.

'Perhaps,' she said now, aware of him watching her. 'But at the time I wasn't thinking very coherently, I suppose.'

'And you knew your father wouldn't have approved,' put in Remy, putting his hand across the table and capturing her wrist. 'Don't worry. I'm coming to terms with your loyalty. I guess that's what I really wanted to say.'

Megan's throat felt tight. His fingers gripping her wrist were strong and strangely comforting, and for the first time she acknowledged to herself that perhaps she hadn't made a mistake in coming here. Maybe this was what she needed—this feeling of family. This awareness that people cared about her, in spite of everything.

And then she permitted herself to meet his eyes and changed her mind again. However appealing it might seem, she was not here to share her problems with him. Apart from anything else, he was far too familiar, and much too disturbing to her peace of mind.

She was about to draw her hand away, when Remy blew out a breath and said, almost casually, 'I guess Mom told you that Pops is dying, didn't she?' He watched her eyes widen, and then added flatly, 'I know. I'm not supposed to know.'

Megan stared at him. 'But then how—how did you—?'

'Mom thinks it's a big secret,' he went on, without answering her. 'But I'm not as dumb as all that.' He grimaced.

'Goddammit, Megan, that's why they invited you here. He wants to ask your forgiveness. Why else would he want to do that?'

CHAPTER FOUR

'HE WANTS to ask my forgiveness?'

Megan was stunned. Anita hadn't even suggested that her father might be having a crisis of conscience, and she wasn't altogether sure she believed it. After all, Ryan hadn't considered her feelings when he'd destroyed her parents' marriage, so why should he care whether she forgave him now?

'I guess he never did get over the guilt he felt about your mother losing her daughter,' Remy offered gently. 'He's not a bad old guy really, whatever you may have been told.'

'Whatever *my father* told me,' Megan said tightly, pressing her shoulders back against the chair. She shook her head, and looked down at his hand clasping hers. 'Remy, I don't think—'

'Don't think,' he advised her softly, massaging her knuckles with his thumb. 'I find it's better not to pre-judge a situation. That way, you can't be accused of being partisan.'

'But aren't you being partisan?' she protested, only too aware of the faint roughness of his skin abrading hers. 'Obviously you're more prepared to see your grandfather's side of things than me.'

'Why?' Remy sighed. 'Because I'm trying to persuade you that there are two sides to every situation?'

Megan took a steadying breath, intensely conscious of the fact that her sensitivity to his touch was in danger of colouring her judgement. How easy it would be, she thought, to turn her hand and link her fingers with his, to feel the heat of his palm hot against her own...

'Things aren't always that simple, Megan,' he persisted, and she forced herself to concentrate on what he was saying. 'You should know that. I mean—who'd have thought you'd be holding my hand like this when only yesterday you were accusing me of giving you a hard time—?'

'Why, you—'

Megan would have withdrawn her hand then, but as if anticipating her reaction he only laughed and held it even tighter. 'That's better,' he said, as her eyes sparkled with resentment, and then his expression altered, and he muttered, 'Oh, hell!' before letting her go.

His sudden exclamation and the scowl that accompanied it were so unexpected that even though he had released her hand she didn't immediately take it back. It was obvious that something, or someone, was responsible for his sudden change of mood, but when he abruptly swung himself to his feet she could only stare at him with bemused eyes.

'My mother,' he explained in an undertone, and Megan barely had time to absorb that information before Anita herself appeared from behind the trellis.

'Why, Remy!' she said, much as she had done the night before, and Megan was uneasily aware that she wasn't pleased. 'I didn't realise you two had arranged to meet for breakfast.' She gave Megan a determined smile. 'Did you have a good night?'

'I didn't—that is—' Megan caught Remy's eye and revised her explanation. 'I slept very well, thank you,' she said instead, even though she hadn't really. 'Um—it's a beautiful morning, isn't it? Too nice to stay in bed.'

'All our mornings are beautiful mornings here,' said Anita crisply, and Megan had the feeling it was her standard response to that kind of remark. She turned to her son. 'What time did you arrive? I didn't hear the car. You might have told me you were here. This is my home, you know.'

Remy's mouth turned down. 'Gee, and I was treating it like a hotel,' he said drily, earning another reproving look from his mother. 'I didn't intend to go without seeing you. But—well, Megan was already here, and we got talking.'

'What about?'

Anita's tone was clipped, and Megan wondered if her

stepsister had sensed the disturbing air of intimacy between them. But who was she kidding? she asked herself, a few moments later. Remy had been friendly, that was all. She shouldn't read too much into his words.

'This and that.' Remy was annoyingly oblique. 'How's the old man this morning? Have you seen him? I thought I'd drop by and see how he is before I go.'

Anita's expression slackened. 'He's—as well as can be expected, I suppose. But I'd rather you didn't disturb him this morning, Remy. I don't want him to get too excited before he meets Megan.'

Remy's lips twisted. 'Since when did seeing me excite him?'

'Well, I don't want to take the risk,' declared his mother firmly. 'You can see him later. You and Rachel are joining us for dinner this evening, aren't you?'

'Maybe.'

'There you are then.' Anita was struggling to be pleasant. 'And your grandfather's looked forward so much to Megan's coming. You never know, it might make all the difference.'

'I doubt it.'

Remy was laconic, and Anita's eyes glittered with obvious irritation. 'We don't know,' she insisted, her dark head tilted at an impatient angle. 'He's frail, I know, but he's stable. The doctor says—'

'That he could have a relapse at any time,' Remy finished for her. 'Don't give me platitudes, Mom. I know.'

'You know?' Anita made a valiant attempt to appear nonplussed. 'What do you know?'

'I know the old man's dying,' Remy stated flatly. 'What did you think? I couldn't see what was happening for myself?'

Anita's eyes turned to Megan now, and Megan felt as if she was being accused of betraying a sacred trust. 'He—he did know,' she offered lamely, but she had the feeling that Anita didn't believe her.

'How did you find out?' she asked her son abruptly, and

Megan was glad she was still sitting, and didn't have to confront her stepsister on her feet.

'I asked the doctor,' replied Remy without flinching. 'Unlike you, he treated me as an adult.'

Anita's shoulders sagged then, and, casting a half-apologetic glance in Megan's direction, she pulled out a chair from the table and sank into it. 'I wish you'd told me,' she said, looking up at him, and Megan remembered what she'd said about bearing the burden alone.

'You should have told me,' retorted Remy, straightening the lapel of his jacket.

'But you're so young,' his mother murmured, biting her lower lip. 'I didn't think it was fair to put it on you. You've got problems of your own. I didn't want you to have to worry about your grandfather as well.'

Remy's nostrils flared. 'Well...' It was obvious he would have liked to say more, but a glance at his watch provided an alternative escape. 'I'd better go. What time do you want us tonight? About seven?'

Anita nodded. 'Seven, yes. We'll eat about seven-thirty, if there are no hold-ups.' She turned to Megan, and forced a smile. 'I always cross my fingers. As I said last night, it's one of the joys of running a hotel.'

Ryan Robards occupied one of the hotel's bungalows.

Set in the grounds, some distance from the hotel proper, the single-storey villas provided families with the alternative of either using the hotel's facilities or catering for themselves. Each bungalow contained a living room and kitchen, with either one or two bedrooms. Self-catered meals were generally taken on the verandahs that wrapped around three sides of the bungalows, where guests could enjoy the view of the beach and the ocean beyond.

On their way there later in the morning, Anita explained that it was easier to take care of her father away from the noise of the hotel itself. 'I suppose he should be in the hospital,' she said, 'but I know he'd hate that. He does have full-time nursing care, and his nurse can reach me any time of the day or night.'

'It sounds like the ideal solution to me,' said Megan, grateful of anything to distract her thoughts from the prospect of the interview ahead. 'Um—so have you—have you spoken to him this morning? Are you sure that he wants to see me?'

'I'm sure.'

But Anita didn't elaborate, and Megan could hardly confront her stepsister with what Remy had said. She still couldn't believe what he'd told her in any case. Her memories of Ryan Robards did not encourage her to take a sympathetic view.

Her first impressions were overlaid with the pervasive odour of the sickroom. It was a distinctive smell, a combination of medication and disinfectant which, even with the air-conditioning, still created a kind of enclosed atmosphere. The sense of airlessness was enhanced by the oxygen mask covering Ryan's face. Obviously he had difficulty breathing, and in spite of herself Megan was disturbed.

He had changed so much. He'd lost an awful lot of weight, and when he saw them and dragged the mask away from his nose she was shocked by the gauntness of his features. She remembered a big man, strong and muscular, whose boisterous laugh had made everyone want to join in. This man was just a shadow of the man her mother had fallen in love with, a pale reflection of the individual her father had declared had ruined his life.

The arms lying on the sheet were thin and lifeless, the folds of skin evidence of the flesh that had melted away. Even his hands were thin and bony, the nails unexpectedly long and curved like talons.

But the eyes that sought her face were anything but lifeless. They burned in his wasted features with an unexpectedly vivid fire. 'Meggie,' he said, gazing at her almost hungrily. 'I'm so glad you agreed to come.'

Megan didn't know what to say. The male nurse, who had been tidying the room when they arrived, had disappeared, and when Megan glanced around, seeking Anita's support she found she had left her, too. She was alone with Ryan Robards, alone with the man she had never allowed herself to regard as her stepfather—the man her father had taught her to hate.

She swallowed. 'Mr Robards.' She acknowledged his greeting politely. 'How—how are you?'

It was an unnecessary question, perhaps, but it was hard to think of anything else to say. She could hardly thank him for inviting her, when he must know she had come here under duress.

He coughed before answering her, a thick, wheezing cough that had him seeking the relief of the oxygen mask before he was able to go on. 'I've been better,' he croaked at last, with a trace of humour. 'But thank you for asking. Even though I guess you don't really give a damn how I feel.'

'That's not true—' began Megan quickly, and then halted at the cynical expression that crossed his face. 'I mean, I'd feel sorry for anyone who—who—'

'Was dying?' he suggested drily, and Megan felt the heat of embarrassment flooding her cheeks.

'Who's ill,' she corrected stiffly, even if he patently didn't believe her. 'I had no idea—that is, Anita didn't tell me that—that you weren't—still—running the hotel.'

'Oh, bravo!' His response was vaguely mocking, and he made a gallant effort to applaud. 'It's hard to find the right words, isn't it?' he got out hoarsely, before once again taking refuge in the mask. Then, after a moment, he said, 'I guess it took a lot of spunk to come here.'

Spunk? Megan considered the word carefully. Spunk meant courage, and she would never have regarded herself as courageous. On the contrary, she thought of herself as something of a moral coward. After all, she'd really only come because Anita had invited her, and she hadn't been able to think of a convincing excuse.

'It's been a long time,' she said, moving a little closer to the bed. Then, because his intent gaze disturbed her, she added awkwardly, 'It's been good to see Anita and—and Remy again.'

'Good for them, too,' he assured her harshly, before another spasm of coughing racked his narrow frame. His lips quivered. 'Did anyone ever tell you you're the image of your mother at the same age?'

Megan blew out a breath. 'Anita said that.'

'She would.' He pressed a fist against his chest, and for a moment she thought he had forgotten she was there. 'We had so little time together,' he breathed unsteadily. 'I loved her so much...' He swallowed convulsively. 'I miss her still.'

Megan's hands came together, her fingers linking and unlinking as she tried to reconcile her memories of this man with the broken individual she saw before her. She watched as a tear escaped from the corner of his eye and trickled slowly down his cheek, and in spite of herself she felt as if a hand was squeezing her heart. Whatever her father had thought, whatever he had said, there seemed little doubt in her mind that Ryan really had loved her mother, and their relationship had not just been the result of a reckless passion that had destroyed lives without thought or conscience.

But, as if assuming that he was embarrassing her, Ryan smudged a hand across his eyes and forced another smile. 'I'm sorry,' he said. 'I'm not usually so maudlin. It's all the drugs they pump into you these days. I doubt if there's any part of my system that hasn't been artificially resuscitated.'

Megan's lips parted. 'Well, at least you have a beautiful place to recuperate in,' she ventured at last, wishing Anita would come back. 'I think the improvements you've made to the hotel are excellent. And—and my rooms are—terrific.'

'You're comfortable?'

'Very.'

'That's good.'

But Ryan's voice was much fainter now, and Megan guessed that talking so much was exhausting him. Perhaps she should just go, she thought uneasily. What more could he say, after all? He'd told her how much he'd loved her mother, and she was amazed to find that she believed him. It didn't excuse what he'd done, but it did give her a new perspective on the whole affair.

'You'll stay?' he asked, his voice barely audible over the sound of his laboured breathing, and Megan wondered for a moment whether he expected her to stay with him until…until… 'I mean—you'll stay for a few weeks, won't you?' he elaborated weakly. 'I know Anita would appreciate it.'

Megan nodded somewhat jerkily. 'I—of course,' she said quickly, instantly jeopardising any thought she might have had about curtailing her visit. 'If I can.'

'Good. Good.'

He closed his eyes then, his breathing deepening, and, realising she could leave, Megan turned somewhat blindly for the door. It wasn't until she got outside that she realised there were tears on her cheeks, too, and she scrubbed at them with an impatient hand. Heavens, she thought, and she had been so sure that nothing Ryan Robards said or did could affect her. How wrong she had been.

'All right?'

It was Anita at last, appearing from the direction of the kitchen, her sharp eyes missing nothing of Megan's distress. What had she expected? Megan wondered. That she wouldn't be moved by Ryan's condition, or that, like her father, she'd be unable to forget the past?

'He's asleep,' she said obliquely, and Anita's shoulders sagged a little.

'You spoke to him?'

'Briefly,' Megan conceded. She took a deep breath. 'Do you think we could go now?'

'Oh, yes.' Anita took a moment to check that her father really was sleeping, and then led the way out onto the sun-drenched verandah. 'I forgot how harrowing his condition must seem to someone who hasn't seen him for such a long time.' She gave a wry grimace. 'I'm used to it and actually he's a little better this morning, believe it or not.'

Megan shook her head. 'I'm so sorry,' she said, not knowing what else to say. 'But it must be some relief to know now that Remy understands.'

'Do you think so?' Anita sounded doubtful. 'The doctor says he has only a few weeks left.' They started back towards the hotel, and her lips twisted ruefully. 'You've no idea how hard it's been to hide my feelings. Remy's my son, and I suppose I still regard him as a child.'

Megan bit her lip. 'You should have called me sooner.'

Anita turned to look at her. 'You don't mind?'

Megan shook her head. 'How could I mind?' She put aside her own misgivings. 'And you should have told me why—why your father wanted to see me.'

Anita's eyes darkened. 'He told you?'

Megan coloured, realising she had almost betrayed something Remy had told her in confidence. 'Um—who?' she asked innocently, and Anita's eyes narrowed.

'Why, Pops of course,' she said, and Megan swallowed.

'He told me he was pleased to see me,' she said awkwardly, aware of the guilty colour in her cheeks. She hesitated. 'Is that what you mean?'

Anita frowned, and then, as if thinking better of probing deeper, she returned her attention to the path ahead. 'I suppose so,' she said a little tightly. 'I know it must have been hard for him, seeing you, in spite of what he said. It must have brought back so many memories of your mother.'

'Yes.' The lump was back in Megan's throat. 'He said—he said he'd loved her very much.'

'He did.' Anita's tone was almost bitter. 'More than—more than you will ever know.'

Megan had the feeling that that wasn't what she had wanted to say, but she'd avoided any reference to Giles Cross. 'So,' Anita added as they approached the entrance to the hotel, 'I hope you'll feel able to visit him again.'

Megan was tempted to ask, Why? but she didn't. She would wait and see whether what Remy had intimated was true. Despite what she'd said, she wasn't absolutely sure that Anita trusted her. And why should she? Megan was her father's daughter, after all.

'Well...' Anita halted in the airy foyer and made a concerted effort to behave normally. 'Have you any plans for the rest of the day?'

Megan glanced at her watch. 'Oh—I thought I might have a rest this afternoon,' she offered. 'I think the time change is getting to me. I am—rather weary.'

'Of course. You must be.' Anita seized on the idea with obvious relief. 'And this evening you'll join us for dinner, won't you? I know Remy will want to introduce you to Rachel. And I'll be glad to have someone of my own age to talk to. So often with those two I feel like the skeleton at the feast.'

Megan pressed her lips together. 'Oh, I'm sure that's not true,' she protested, aware that once again Anita was making a distinction between them and her son. 'Anyway—' she forced a smile '—I'll look forward to it.'

'So will I,' Anita agreed, and then, as one of the hotel employees came purposefully towards them, added, 'You'll excuse me now, Megan? This looks like trouble.'

CHAPTER FIVE

'WHAT'S wrong?' Rachel De Vries nestled closer to Remy's shoulder, the solid console of the open-topped buggy preventing her from getting any nearer. She tilted her head, and her long curly hair swung against the sleeve of his shirt, a dark contrast to the cream silk. 'Is it your mother?'

'Nothing's wrong.' Remy glanced affectionately down at her, hoping she wouldn't press him all the same. 'I was thinking, that's all.'

'You've been thinking all the way from Port Serrat, then,' said Rachel drily, lifting her head and sitting up straighter in her seat. 'If I've done something wrong, tell me. I don't want to spend the evening wondering what it is.'

'It's nothing, I've told you,' declared Remy shortly, aware that his tone was sharper than it should be. 'I've got a lot on my mind at the moment, Rachel. What with the Rainbird trial and Pops' illness.'

'I know, I know.' Rachel gave a placatory wave of her hand, and smoothed the skirt of her dress. Short, like most of the clothes she wore, the lemon-yellow print flared about her thighs, exposing her slim legs, of which she was justifiably proud. 'I'm just nervous, I suppose. I'm not looking forward to meeting this—surrogate aunt of yours.'

Remy's lips tightened. 'She's not a surrogate aunt.'

'All right, your step-aunt, then. What does it matter?' She made a sound of impatience. 'I just think it's kind of morbid. Turning up here when your grandfather is dying.'

'She didn't just turn up here,' declared Remy doggedly. 'You know very well that my mother invited her. And Pops

58

wanted to see her, too. It's really down to him that she's here at all.'

'Mmm.' Rachel's lips curled unpleasantly. 'All the same, it's funny that she's accepted your mother's invitation now, after all these years. Is she hoping he'll remember her in his will?'

'I doubt it.'

Remy was abrupt, and he couldn't help wondering why the things Rachel was saying irritated him so much. When he'd first heard that Megan was coming here, he'd been sceptical, too. Only the knowledge that she'd been seriously ill had persuaded him to keep his comments to himself.

And then, when he'd met her...

'So what's she like?' Rachel persisted. 'You've not said very much about her, I must say. All I know is that she's half a dozen years or so younger than your mother, and that she nearly died from a perforated ulcer.'

Remy sighed. 'What do you want to know?' he asked patiently. 'She's fairly tall—taller than you, anyway—and she's very thin. She's a blonde, so naturally she's pale-skinned, and her eyes are blue. Is that good enough for you?'

Rachel grimaced. 'That's not what I meant, actually.' But, as if realising she was being less than charitable, she took a more optimistic tone. 'I just wondered if I'd like her, that's all.'

'I'm sure you will,' said Remy tersely, cursing as a reckless motorcyclist cut across him at a junction. 'Now, can we talk about something else?'

Rachel gave him a curious look. 'If you say so,' she agreed, pleating the hem of her skirt. 'What?'

Remy was impatient. 'What—what?'

'What do you want to talk about?'

Remy blew out a breath. 'I don't know, do I? Anything; everything.' He paused. 'Has your sister heard yet how she did in her exams?'

'Now, I'm sure you're not really interested in how Ruth did in her mid-term exams,' declared Rachel mildly. And then, at his hard stare, she said, 'She did all right as it happens. Nothing to worry about. Okay?'

'Okay.'

'What is it with you?' Remy was unhappily aware that his attitude was not helping his case. 'Come on, Remy. I know you too well.'

Remy was ruefully coming to the conclusion that she didn't know him at all. Unfortunately, he had the same feeling about himself, and he realised he might have stretched his own credibility by coming here tonight.

'I've told you,' he said, his smile grim even by his own standards. 'I'm tired, I guess.' He hesitated, and then continued honestly, 'I'm not looking forward to this evening either.'

He bit back the words 'But for different reasons,' and was relieved to see that Rachel seemed to take what he'd said at face value.

'Your mother,' she murmured sympathetically, leaning towards him again and squeezing his muscled forearm. She dimpled. 'Doesn't she know we're practically living together? All she ever talks about is when we're going to get married. I know she wants grandchildren. I want children, too. But not yet.'

Remy's mouth tightened. 'She's old-fashioned,' he said flatly. 'And we haven't exactly set up house together.'

'But we will,' said Rachel impatiently. 'Eventually. I'll be twenty-one in six weeks' time, and then Daddy won't have any say in where I choose to live.'

'Perhaps not.'

Remy knew he sounded unsympathetic now, but he'd been having some misgivings about Rachel's idea of moving in together. He liked her a lot; dammit, he was very fond of her; but she was still very young, and he didn't just mean in years. As the youngest member of the De Vries family, she was used to getting her own way in everything, and that, combined with her youth, often created friction between them.

'You don't sound very enthusiastic!' she exclaimed petulantly, flinging herself back in her seat again. 'Honestly, sometimes I wonder why I put up with your moods!'

'With my moods?' Remy was sardonic. 'Oh, please.'

'Well—' Rachel sniffed. 'It's not my fault if your mother's always on your case. Usually it's the hotel she wants you for, but now it's this—woman. This long-lost relative who's getting up your nose.'

'Megan is not getting up my nose,' retorted Remy grimly, annoyed at how much he resented her words. 'For heaven's sake, I'm tired. How many more times do I have to say it? I need a break, for God's sake. I've been working flat out since Thanksgiving.'

Rachel looked for a minute as if she might take exception to his tirade, but then his outburst seemed to remind her of something else. Snatching up her purse, she rummaged in the pocket for a few moments, uttering a triumphant cry when she found the scrap of paper she'd been looking for.

'Talking of breaks,' she said delightedly, waving the paper in his face, 'I got that information you wanted about Orruba. The next charter boat leaves two weeks from Thursday, and, as you expected, they supply all the equipment. How does a couple of weeks' treasure-hunting appeal to you?'

Megan sat on her balcony as long as she dared, putting off the moment when she would have to go in and get changed. She'd had her shower earlier, and all she had to do was put on some make-up and get dressed, but the prospect of the evening ahead was not appealing. Despite Anita's kindness to her, she was very much aware of being the outsider here, and she suspected she would have preferred to recuperate among people she didn't know.

Or was that being entirely honest? Was it not more to the point to say that she would have preferred not to spend the evening with Remy and his fiancée? It wasn't that she had anything against the girl. On the contrary, she was prepared to accept Anita's word that Rachel was one of the sweetest young women you could meet. But she—

Megan—didn't belong here, whatever the Robards said, and she was sure it would have been easier for all of them if she'd maintained the status quo.

Of course, she knew she was being ungrateful. But by accepting their invitation she had put herself into their hands. Or rather by Simon's accepting on her behalf, she thought wryly. She would have a few choice words to say to her business partner when she got back.

The phone rang at that moment. The distinctive sound carried easily onto the balcony, and, guessing it was Anita, making sure she wouldn't be late for dinner, Megan got unwillingly to her feet and padded indoors.

'Hello,' she said, instantly aware of a certain hollowness on the line, and then, as if her thoughts had conjured the man, she heard Simon Chater's voice.

'Hi, Megs,' he said, using his own affectionate name for her. 'I hoped I'd catch you before you went down for dinner. I'm just on my way to bed myself.'

Megan caught her breath. 'Simon!' she exclaimed, the warmth of her tone in direct contrast to the thoughts she'd been having earlier. 'Oh, gosh, I promised to ring you, didn't I? But there's been so much going on, I'm afraid I forgot.'

'No problem.' Simon was unperturbed. 'But I'm glad to hear you arrived safely. So—how are you? How are you feeling? Has the long-awaited reunion taken place?'

'I don't know what long-awaited reunion you're referring to,' said Megan tartly, 'but yes, I've met all my step-relatives again.'

'That's good.' Simon sounded pleased. 'I told you you'd enjoy it once you were there.'

'Did I say I was enjoying it?' countered Megan drily. But then, half afraid that someone might be listening in, she amended her words. 'It's a beautiful place,' she agreed, without committing herself. 'And—and Anita and her family have been very kind.'

'Anita? That's the woman I spoke to, isn't it?'

'That's right.' Megan did her best not to allow her own

misgivings to show. 'And there's her son, Remy, and—and my stepfather, Ryan Robards. Only unfortunately he's very ill.'

'Your stepfather?'

'Yes.' Megan was amazed at how quickly she had adapted to a relationship that she'd always denied existed. 'It's been very hard for Anita coping alone.'

'But she has a son, doesn't she?' Simon pointed out. 'And however young he was when you last saw him he must be in his twenties now.'

'Yes, he is.' Megan bit her lip. 'But—well, I suppose it's different having someone of your own generation to talk to. I'm more Anita's age; Remy isn't.'

'You're not old enough to have a son of that age!' exclaimed Simon, with a short laugh. 'I know you've been looking pretty grim lately, Megs, but get a grip.'

Megan felt a rueful smile tugging at her lips. It was good to talk to Simon again, she reflected. At least he could be relied on to put things into perspective.

'Anyway, you still haven't told me how you're feeling,' he continued. 'I hope you're taking it easy. I expect you to have an all-over tan when you get back.'

Megan chuckled. 'I'll do my best.' She shook her head. 'It's so good to hear from you, Simon. I didn't realise how much I'd missed your sarcastic voice.'

They spoke a little longer about business matters: how the launch was going in New York, for example, and the tentative enquiry they'd had from Australia. Megan felt a brief wave of homesickness sweep over her as they talked about the new season's designs and the feedback they'd had from the public. This was her world, she thought impatiently. She'd soon be bored living here with nothing to do.

Indeed, in spite of what she'd told Simon, as soon as he rang off she wondered how she was going to face the next four weeks. She simply wasn't a hedonist; she couldn't remember when she'd last taken a holiday. And with only Anita for company the days were going to seem awfully long.

But, as she prepared for dinner, she admitted that taking a break hadn't exactly been an option. Going back to work too early could easily wreck her recovery. She needed to rest; to recuperate. To regain her strength for the taxing months ahead.

She examined her appearance critically before going downstairs. The bronze Chinese silk shirt, with its bands of black and gold and red, was loose enough to draw attention away from the narrowness of the matching ankle-length skirt. It, too, was banded around the hem, and she slipped her feet into a pair of black heel-less court shoes. They added to her height, and she was glad of that. She was used to being on eye-level terms with most of the men of her acquaintance, and Remy topped her by some half a dozen inches.

She still looked pale, even after the careful application of some blusher, but she doubted anyone would notice. The advantages of eating by candlelight were not just nostalgic, she thought as she went down in the lift with a group of American tourists who were apparently on their way to the Harbour Bar.

Megan got out of the lift at the mezzanine, and walked across the reception area to the door leading into Anita's private apartments. A couple of the young women on the reception desk gave her a friendly smile, and she guessed they had already been told who she was. She closed the door behind her, and then, squaring her shoulders, she started down the corridor to the sitting room. She just hoped Anita was already there tonight. It might be awkward meeting Remy if she wasn't.

She was. Dressed in a navy taffeta cocktail dress, Anita was seated on the sofa beside a very pretty dark-haired girl wearing a yellow floral mini-dress. Remy was lounging in an armchair opposite, and they all looked towards the door as Megan made her entrance.

Despite her determination not to let them disconcert her, it was an awkward moment. Whether it was the perceptive glance Remy cast his fiancée, or the significant way both women stopped talking and studied her appearance, Megan didn't know, but there was no doubt that her arrival had created a vacuum.

Remy was the first to recover, getting easily to his feet and bidding her to sit down. 'Mineral water?' he suggested, proving he'd remembered their encounter of the night before, and Megan nodded gratefully as Anita made the introductions.

Megan had the feeling her stepsister had expected Remy to introduce the two younger women, but his offer of a drink was deliberate. Consequently, it was left to Anita to do the honours, and Megan shook hands with Rachel before taking a seat.

'How are you feeling now?' Anita asked, as if Megan's health had been under discussion. She turned to the girl beside her. 'I expect Remy told you it was touch-and-go for a while.'

'Oh, I—' Megan started, but before she could say anything in her own defence Rachel chimed in.

'Oh, yes,' she said, sympathetically. 'He said you'd come here to recuperate after an operation. I can't imagine what it must be like to have an ulcer!' She gave a delicate shudder. 'I hope it's a long time before I find out.'

'I hope you never find out,' declared Anita firmly, patting Rachel's hand in a proprietorial way. She smiled. 'Thankfully, we don't have the pressures here that Megan has, do we, dear?'

'Well—' began Megan again, but this time Remy intervened.

'You make it sound as if everyone who lives in London is living on a knife-edge,' he remarked drily, handing Megan a glass containing ice and mineral water before resuming his seat. 'As I understand it, ulcers can be caused in various ways. Stress isn't always the reason.'

'It usually is,' declared his mother, but Megan had heard enough.

'Do you think we could talk about something else?' she asked, not enjoying being the centre of attention. She looked at Rachel pleasantly. 'Have you lived on San Felipe all your life?'

'I'm afraid so.' Rachel's words were innocent enough but she didn't sound apologetic. 'Remy and I are both native islanders. I don't think either of us could bear to live anywhere else.'

'No.'

Megan acknowledged the truth of that as she sipped some of the chilled water in her glass. Anita had said much the same thing when she had spoken so proudly of the opportunities Remy had rejected on the mainland. Even when she was dying, her mother had said that San Felipe got into your blood.

'Anita was telling me that you run a fashion catalogue,' Rachel put in now, and Megan schooled her features into a polite mask.

'It's a directory, actually,' she said. 'We don't sell the clothes ourselves. We just provide a showcase for amateur designers—college graduates and the like.'

'It sounds fascinating,' said Anita, but Megan sensed she wasn't really interested in that side of her life. 'But haven't you ever wanted to get married? To settle down and have a family of your own?'

'Not yet,' replied Megan evenly, and the older woman shook her head.

'Well, you're not getting any younger, my dear,' she declared. 'The old body clock is ticking, as they say.'

'Mom!' Remy's impatience was evident, and his mother gave him a defiant look.

'Well, this young man Megan lives with sounds very nice, I must say,' she retorted. 'If I were her, I wouldn't wait much longer to tie him down.'

'Simon and I—' Megan found herself on the brink of disclaiming their association, and then once again decided not to say anything more. After all, what did it matter what the Robards thought about her relationships? In a few weeks' time, they'd have forgotten all about her. 'We're good friends.'

Anita snorted now. 'Good friends!' she exclaimed. 'I've heard that before. Well—' she acknowledged her son's glowering face with a defensive shrug '—I suppose you know your own business best.'

'Yes, she does,' said Remy, finishing his drink and getting up to get himself another. 'And she isn't on the verge of senility either.'

'I never said she was—'

'Tell us how you started the catal—the directory,' said Rachel hurriedly, before her fiancé and his mother could come to verbal blows. 'How did you know where to look for designers?'

'Oh—' Megan's face was uncomfortably hot, but she forced herself to go on. 'It was Simon's idea. He—er—he was working for one of the tabloid newspapers, and during the course of a feature he was writing he visited several art colleges and saw the work they were producing. He realised there was an awful lot of talent going to waste. We decided to provide a showcase for that talent, that's all.'

'But it is clothes we're talking about, isn't it?'

'Mostly.' Megan once again found herself the cynosure of all eyes. 'Occasionally we add a small household section. There's quite a market for soft furnishing fabrics and so on.'

'And who chooses what goes into the—the directory and what doesn't?' asked Anita, with a frown, and Megan sighed.

'We both do,' she replied carefully. 'It's very much a personal point of view.'

'But you've obviously been successful,' pointed out Anita. 'Is that because you and Simon have similar views?'

'It's more because we share a similar eye for colour,' Megan amended quietly. 'Apart from our work, we have very little in common.'

'Oh, I can't believe that.'

Anita was patently disbelieving, and Megan knew she had to change the subject before she said something she'd regret. 'It's true,' she affirmed, and then turned deter-

minedly to the young woman sitting beside her. 'What do
you do—er—Rachel? Do you work in Port Serrat, too?'

'What do I do?' Rachel looked at her now as if she'd
used a dirty word. 'What do I *do*?' She glanced at Remy,
as if expecting him to answer the question for her. 'I
don't—do—anything, if you mean as a way of earning
money. Daddy wouldn't allow it.' She cast a helpless
glance at Anita. 'He's terribly old-fashioned, as you know.'

'He's a dinosaur,' agreed Remy laconically, earning himself another warning look from his mother. 'Well, he is,'
he persisted, coming back to his chair to sit with his legs
splayed, the glass suspended from both hands between
them. 'He's still living in the nineteenth century. He thinks
women were born to breed and nothing else.'

'Remy!'

'Oh, Remy!'

Anita and Rachel spoke together, the former with re-
proval, the latter with a coy little laugh. For her part, Megan
was beginning to wish she had confessed to having a headache and got out of this dinner party. She wasn't enjoying
herself, and she suspected no one but Anita was either.

To her relief, the uniformed waiter who had served them
the night before appeared at that moment to advise her stepsister that the meal was ready to be served. Finishing her
sherry, Anita got immediately to her feet, and, tucking her
arm through Rachel's, she led the way out onto the terrace.

Megan put down her own glass and followed them, the
distinctive sound of a steel band becoming audible as she
stepped outside. A barbecue was taking place on the beach,
and she could smell the spicy food and see the torches that
illuminated the scene. If only she could join that anonymous crowd, she thought wryly. This was supposed to be
a holiday, not an endurance test.

'Bored?' asked a lazy voice far too close to her ear, and
she realised that she had halted for a moment and Remy
had come up behind her. 'Cheer up,' he added. 'It'll soon
be over. You'll have to forgive my mother. She doesn't

realise that dinner guests are supposed to have something in common.'

Megan's lips twitched, but happily the darkness hid her guilty humour. 'I don't know what you mean,' she insisted, moving quickly towards the candlelit table. She admired the pretty centre-piece of ivory orchids and crimson hibiscus. 'This looks lovely, Anita.'

Her stepsister was pleased and the food, as always, was delicious. A light consommé was followed by tender medallions of pork in a sweet and sour sauce, served on a bed of flaky rice, with a delicate fruit terrine to finish. Megan realised as the plates were cleared that despite her reservations she had enjoyed the meal. Probably because Rachel and Anita had done most of the talking, she acknowledged drily. Her contributions had been few and far between, which suited her very well.

It was as Anita was pouring cups of aromatic Colombian coffee that once again Remy chose to disrupt her mood. 'You saw Pops this morning?' he enquired, cutting across his mother's dissertation on what a mischievous little boy he used to be, and there was a moment's awkward silence before anyone spoke.

And then it was Anita who chose to answer him, her eyes sparkling impatiently, as if she'd hoped to avoid this discussion. 'Of course she saw your grandfather,' she declared tersely. 'What kind of a question is that?'

Remy shrugged his shoulders, and Megan looked away from the sleek muscles moving under brown skin. He was wearing a cream shirt this evening, and his tan showed darkly beneath the fine silk. 'I was talking to Megan actually,' he said, his tone bordering on insolence. 'Well?' He fixed her with a taut gaze. 'What did he have to say?'

Megan was again glad of the darkness to hide her blushes. What was wrong with her, she wondered, that he should have the ability to embarrass her without any apparent effort on his part? 'He—said he was glad to see me,' she answered at last, exchanging an apologetic look with

Anita. 'He said I was like—like my mother. I think seeing me was—was rather painful for him.'

'I'll bet.' To her relief Remy seemed content with her answer. He bit his lip. 'I'll look in on him myself before I leave.'

'Can I come, too?'

Rachel, who was seated at right angles to Remy, covered the hand that was playing with the stem of his wine glass with her own, but he shook his head. 'I don't think so,' he said, raising the glass to his lips so that her fingers were forced to fall away. 'Doc O'Brien's orders are only family.' His smile was faintly malicious. 'And you're not that—yet.'

Rachel's response was to thrust back her chair and leave the table. As Megan and Anita exchanged helpless glances, she rushed indoors and out of their sight. No one was in any doubt that Remy's words had upset her, and as soon as she was sure the girl was out of earshot Anita turned on her son.

'There was no need for that!' she exclaimed, screwing up her napkin and thrusting it to one side. 'You know perfectly well that what Dr O'Brien meant was that your grandfather shouldn't have a lot of visitors. Allowing Rachel to accompany you would have done no harm at all.'

Remy tilted his chair onto the two back legs and gazed carelessly at the star-studded heavens. 'Perhaps I didn't want her to go with me,' he declared, and his mother made a sound of impatience.

'You're being deliberately unpleasant, Remy,' she retorted, almost as if he were still the small boy she had been speaking about earlier. 'Now for goodness' sake go and tell the girl you're sorry. I can hear her sniffling away in the sitting room and I know it's not because she's coming down with a cold.'

Remy's chair legs dropped with ominous speed, and Megan wished she were any place but here. But her only obvious exit was through the room where Rachel was hiding, and she had no wish to embarrass the girl any more than she already was.

'I'm not a child, Mom,' Remy stated now, his eyes meeting his mother's bleakly across the table. 'And I object to you behaving as if my relationship with Rachel was a *fait accompli*.' He paused. 'It's not. All right?'

Anita's lips quivered. 'You're just saying that to punish me.'

'No, I'm not.' Remy caught Megan's eyes upon him, and she quickly looked down at her cup. 'And I suggest you tell Megan why she's really here, instead of pretending it's just because of the old man's health!'

CHAPTER SIX

MEGAN put down her book and reached for the tube of sunscreen lying on the low table beside her. Although the lounger she was occupying was shaded by a striped umbrella, as the sun moved round, her legs were becoming exposed, and she could feel the heat of the sun prickling her skin.

Uncapping the tube, she squeezed a circle of the cream onto her palm and applied it to her ankle. She felt an immediate sense of relief as the cream did its work, and she paused a moment to look about her, reluctantly admitting that she was lucky to be in such delightful surroundings.

She was sitting by the hotel pool, another innovation since the days when she and her parents had visited the island. Anita had told her that having a pool was almost mandatory these days. Not all their guests enjoyed getting sand between their toes or combating the flies that occasionally plagued the beach area. Many people, women particularly, only wore a swimsuit for sunbathing. They never went into the water, and although they enjoyed being photographed beside the pool it was more of a decoration than a resource.

For her part, Megan enjoyed both locations. It was true that she preferred to swim in the sea, but so far she hadn't swum at all. She was still very chary about doing anything that might upset her recovery, which was why she was so protective of her skin.

Of course, she had developed a slight tan. Because she endeavoured to spend as much time as possible out of the hotel, it had been impossible to remain totally immune from the effects of sun. She was sure she must have walked miles in her efforts to rebuild her strength—and try to avoid Anita, she admitted with a pang.

Not that she'd been very successful with the latter, she acknowledged ruefully. Apart from anything else, her step-sister insisted that they have their evening meal together, though, thankfully, there'd been no repeat of the disastrous dinner party she'd given five days ago. On the whole, Megan's days had been fairly uneventful, with only her visits to see Ryan Robards making this any different from an ordinary holiday.

Still, just thinking about the evening Remy had brought Rachel to dinner brought an uneasy feathering of her skin. She should have stuck by her instincts and made some excuse not to attend, she reflected wryly. Although she hadn't said anything, Megan was sure Anita blamed her for at least a part of the unpleasantness that had occurred. And it wasn't as if she had wanted to be there. She would have much preferred to eat in the restaurant.

The evening had ended as inauspiciously as it had begun. After Remy's outburst, Anita had gone to attend to Rachel, and Megan had followed her and made good her escape. Neither she nor Anita had mentioned it since, even though it would have been more natural to do so.

Which meant she was no wiser now as to the reason Ryan had wanted to see her than before. There had been no mention of there being another reason why he had wanted her here. Megan sometimes wondered if Remy had made the whole thing up. Or was Anita hoping that no more need be said?

For her part, Megan was inclined to the same view. Although she and Ryan had spoken more in the last few days than they had ever done, their exchanges tended to be more reminiscing about her mother than anything else. How he felt now, what he thought during the long hours he spent alone in his room, seemed of less importance to him than what had gone before. And his memories of Laura were precious—more precious with every hour they spent together.

Feeling the sting of tears behind her eyes, Megan determinedly reached for her sunglasses. She was not going to cry, she told herself. She had done all her crying years ago. But there was no doubt that Ryan had given her a new perspective on the woman who had borne her, and although she still sympathised with her father she was beginning to see that his view had been decidedly biased.

She sank back against the lounger, picking up her paperback again and trying to stimulate some interest in the story. But the characters she was reading about were so two-dimensional, and her mind refused to concentrate on the plot.

She wondered what Remy was doing at this moment, and then swiftly dismissed the thought. The less she saw of her 'nephew' the better, she decided. He'd been around the hotel twice since the evening of the dinner party, but happily she hadn't seen him. He visited his grandfather regularly, but she'd been out both times he'd made the trip from town.

She sighed now, gazing up at the canopy above her head, watching the shadows of the nearby palm trees moving against the cloth. This was a heavenly place, she thought reluctantly. She didn't want to admit it, but she was beginning to understand why her mother had said it got into your blood.

She closed her eyes, only to open them a few seconds later when it seemed as if the sun had been blocked from her view. Despite the sunglasses, she could sense the darkness beyond her eyelids, and she blinked at the man who was standing beside her chair.

It was Remy. Somehow, she'd known it would be, and she wondered if the thoughts she'd had a few moments ago had been inspired by his presence in the hotel. But he was alone; his mother wasn't with him; and Megan was immediately conscious of how unattractive she must appear.

'Hi,' he said, moving her legs aside and perching on the end of the lounger. 'You look hot.'

Megan struggled into a sitting position. 'I am hot,' she

agreed, aware of the layers of sunscreen giving her skin a greasy shine. 'What are you doing here? I thought you'd be working. Or don't lawyers in Port Serrat keep office hours?'

'I neither know nor care what hours other lawyers keep,' declared Remy carelessly, loosening the buttons on his shirt. He pushed back his dark hair with a lazy hand and briefly scanned the poolside area. 'I thought I might keep you company for a while.'

Megan determined not to overreact. 'Is that wise?' she asked, leaning forward to massage an errant drop of cream into her leg. 'I'm sure if your mother knows you're here she'll find something for you to do. She was saying she was having a problem with the coffee machine last night.'

Remy's mouth compressed. 'I'm not an electrician, Megan, and if it's mechanical I'm not an engineer either. My mother knows a perfectly adequate firm of technicians she can call on in an emergency. If she chooses not to use them, that's her problem, not mine.'

'Nevertheless—'

'Nevertheless—what?' Remy stared at her, and she wished she weren't so aware of the muscled expanse of his body visible in the open V of his shirt. 'What is your problem?' he countered. 'Do you object to me being here? I thought you might be glad to see me. It can't be much fun holidaying alone.'

Megan moistened her lips. 'I don't mind what you do,' she protested, not altogether truthfully, but he was not to know that. 'Um—how long are you staying? Is—is Rachel with you?'

Remy gave her a speaking look. 'No, she's not,' he answered at last, though his expression had said it all. 'Rachel and I don't live in one another's pockets, whatever my mother may have told you. She has her friends, I have mine.'

Megan absorbed this. 'But you live together, don't you?' she ventured, needing to know where the younger woman stood.

'Not yet,' replied Remy. 'She lives with her parents. Did my mother tell you otherwise?'

'No,' Megan answered hurriedly. She couldn't let him think Anita had said any such thing. She didn't want him to think they had been talking about him at all. He was far too presumptuous as it was.

'Good.'

Remy got to his feet now, loosening the button at the waistband of the black jeans he was wearing and pulling the ends of his shirt free. Taking it off, he dropped it onto the empty chair beside her, then, leaving her for a moment, he went to take a couple of the courtesy towels from the rack.

He sauntered back casually, dropping the towels beside his shirt before peeling down his jeans. She found herself holding her breath as he disrobed in front of her, but the boxers he was wearing under his jeans were as conventional as shorts.

After spreading the towels, he subsided onto the lounger beside her, and for a while there was silence. The pool deck was only thinly patronised at this hour of the morning, most guests taking advantage of the cooler mornings to go sight-seeing or into town. In consequence, the only sounds were the gentle shushing of the water against the sides of the pool and the occasional whisper of the breeze through the palms.

Megan knew she should have been able to relax again, but she couldn't. Her eyes were irresistibly drawn to the length of the legs residing on the lounger next to her. The fringe of her umbrella hid all but the lower half of his body from her, but what she could see was disturbing and far too interesting for comfort.

She picked up her book again, but it was no use. She read the words over and over again, but they didn't mean anything to her. She actually found herself wondering what it would be like to have a relationship with someone like Remy. She'd never been attracted to young men before, but there was no doubt he was different from the norm…

But he shouldn't be, she reproved herself irritably. For God's sake, what was wrong with her? She was acting as if she'd never seen a man in the nude before. And Remy wasn't nude; he was wearing a perfectly adequate pair of boxers. The fact that they exposed the impressive mound between his legs was purely incidental.

Or it would have been if she hadn't been so curious about him, she realised. He was probably totally unaware of the fact that she was fascinated by his sex. As for Anita— Megan's throat dried. She would be positively appalled if she guessed what Megan was thinking. She'd already made it clear that she considered her her contemporary, not his.

Which was as it should be, Megan told herself, pushing her sunglasses up into her hair and shifting onto her side so she didn't have to look at him. She hitched up the top of her swimsuit, glad that she wasn't wearing anything as revealing as a bikini. But her scar hadn't made that an option, and the terracotta-coloured maillot was happily loose across her taut breasts.

'How are you getting on with the old man now?'

Her restlessness must have communicated itself to him for when she glanced over her shoulder she found he had swung his feet to the ground and was sitting on the edge of his chair.

'Um—we talk,' she said, turning back to the pool again. 'He's easily tired, but I think he likes to see me. We talk a lot about my mother. Sometimes I think he mistakes me for her.'

'Laura.' Remy's voice was low and affectionate, and it did unwelcome things to Megan's senses. 'She was quite a special lady.'

Megan didn't attempt to answer that. She'd changed her mind about a lot of things since she'd been here, but she still felt an instinctive loyalty to her father. Nevertheless, she could see how she might have been mistaken. At fifteen she must have been so naïve.

'How about Mom?' Remy asked. 'How are you getting on with her?' And against her better judgement Megan shifted onto her back.

'We get along fine,' she said, sliding her dark glasses over her eyes, and Remy gave her a knowing look.

'Has she been honest with you yet?' His eyes were intent. 'I know what she's like. She's very good at avoiding awkward subjects.'

'I suppose we all are.'

Megan had spoken carelessly, but now Remy's eyes narrowed. 'What's that supposed to mean?'

Megan's lips parted. 'Nothing.'

'You're not by any chance getting at me?' he countered, and she gave a hurried shake of her head.

'No. Why would I?'

'Who knows?' Remy scowled. 'Something the old man said, perhaps.' He paused. 'Has he mentioned my grandmother to you?'

Megan frowned. 'You don't mean my mother?'

'No. I mean my grandmother,' said Remy flatly. 'His first wife.'

'I'm afraid not.' Megan wondered if that was why he was so irritable suddenly. 'I'm sure he must have loved her, too. But—people get lonely, I suppose.'

Remy's expression was droll. 'I'm not looking for sympathy, you know.'

'I never said you were.' Megan tilted her head. 'I just don't know what you're getting at, that's all.'

'You don't? You mean your father never told you?' Remy's lean features were sceptical. 'I'd have thought that man would have done anything to spite this family.'

Megan stiffened. 'If you're going to start insulting my father again—'

'I'm not.' Remy interrupted her. 'And I promised I'd keep my opinions to myself. But he hurt my mother a lot, and that's not easy to forgive.'

Megan expelled her breath slowly. 'I suppose you mean because he didn't approve of her—keeping you.'

'That was only part of it,' said Remy bitterly. 'But, hey—' his lips tightened '—it's not your concern, is it? I just wanted to know what you were thinking. Whether you felt the same.'

'Felt the same about what?' She frowned.

Remy stared at her. 'It doesn't matter.'

Megan felt confused. 'Is this something to do with *your* father?' she asked cautiously, and then wished she hadn't when his expression grew bleak. 'I don't know what you mean.'

'It doesn't matter,' he said again shortly, and pushed himself to his feet. 'I've disturbed you long enough. I'd better get back.'

'Remy…' Uncaring what he thought of her appearance now, Megan scrambled off the lounger and pulled off the protective glasses. 'Please,' she said, touching his arm, which was rigid with muscle beneath the hair-roughened skin. 'Can't we forget about the past if that's what you're talking about? Or at least not let it influence what happens now?'

Remy looked down at her hand gripping his arm, and then, when she awkwardly withdrew it, he stepped away from her. 'If only we could,' he said drily, stepping into his jeans and pulling up the zip. 'Look, I'd better go and show my face. It wouldn't do for the old lady to think I was avoiding her again.'

Megan knew he was right, but she wondered why that hadn't bothered him earlier. Until she'd implied that everyone had something to hide, they'd been getting along just fine. All right, she'd had her reservations when he'd first appeared, but that was understandable in the circumstances. She was so afraid of betraying herself; so afraid of revealing how attracted to him she was.

Megan chose to have lunch in her room.

She insisted to herself that because she was feeling rather tired she would have done so anyway, but in all honesty she didn't want to intrude on Anita and her son.

It wasn't cowardice, she defended herself, when her conscience pricked her. After her conversation with Remy, she was quite sure he'd be glad not to see her again. For some reason she had offended him when she'd spoken of his father. Why was it such a secret, for heaven's sake? These days being a single mother didn't mean a thing.

Perhaps it was the man himself, she reflected thoughtfully. Perhaps he had treated Anita badly, or refused to accept responsibility for his son. Whatever, it was too long ago now to matter. Surely Remy didn't think it made any difference to her...?

Two more days passed without incident. Simon phoned again to say that all was well in London. He also said he'd met a young man who had some great ideas about next year's directory. He'd suggested that they should consider expanding into the ethnic market. There were so many good Afro-Asian designers with no obvious showcase for their work.

Megan's enthusiasm was lukewarm at best, but she couldn't help it. Despite her determination not to do so, she was becoming involved with the Robards, almost against her will. Ryan's illness and Remy's attitude seemed infinitely more important than next year's fashions. She wouldn't have believed it could happen, but she was no longer counting the days to going back.

Realising she was in danger of stagnating, she decided to ask Anita if she could borrow a car to go into town. She hadn't visited the island's capital since she'd returned to San Felipe, and she also wanted to see the Garden of Remembrance where her mother's ashes had been spread.

She found it wasn't easy, broaching the topic with Anita. Since her arrival, they'd tended to skirt round the details of her mother's death. But her stepsister was quite willing to tell her where the cemetery was, and even offered to go with her if she'd prefer not to risk straining her stomach by driving.

'Oh, I'm sure I'll be fine.' Megan hadn't really considered that possibility, but she'd done so much walking, she was sure she'd be all right. 'And I'd like to go on my own, if you don't mind. It's something I want to do, something I should have done sooner. I hope you understand?'

'Of course.'

Anita didn't argue, and Megan guessed she was hoping it would help her to see Ryan Robards in a more sympathetic light. As far as Megan was concerned, she couldn't wait to get behind the wheel again. It was six weeks since she'd felt in control of her life.

The vehicle Anita lent her was an open-topped buggy, one of several that were available for hire to guests staying at the hotel. Anita also lent her a hat, a floppy-brimmed straw one with a wide scarlet ribbon around the crown, which Megan was rather chary of, but which did a good job of protecting her from the sun.

For the rest, she wore a short pleated skirt in navy, and a short-sleeved shirt. The shirt was a soft lemon silk that accentuated her slight tan, a pair of gold hoops swung from her earlobes, and a matching handful of bangles encircled her wrist.

She was actually feeling much better in herself, she acknowledged with some relief as she drove towards Port Serrat. The weakness she had been suffering when she'd come here was dissipating, and the rest, and the fact that she was eating proper food, instead of just grabbing a sandwich or a takeaway when she could, was bringing the glow of health back to her cheeks. So long as she didn't put on too much weight, she appended. She wanted her clothes to fit her when she got home.

When she got home...

Pausing to allow a man leading an ox-cart that was laden with a wobbly load of green bananas to pull out in front of her, Megan was dismayed to find how reluctant she was to anticipate her return. Like her mother, she was beginning to understand that the island could grow on you, but when had she stopped looking for excuses to leave?

Dismissing such disruptive thoughts, she began to realise how familiar she still was with her surroundings. Although she hadn't been allowed to drive in those days, the holidays she had spent here had given her a comprehensive knowledge of the island. Her father—or her mother—had always hired a car to get about, and they'd often taken Remy with them on their expeditions.

Or at least her mother had, she amended honestly. Giles Cross had not encouraged her friendship with the younger child. Perhaps even then he'd sensed the effect the Robards were going to have on his family, she reflected ruefully. She couldn't believe he had blamed Remy for his mother's sins.

Still, she would never know now, and, putting such thoughts aside, she looked about her with delight. The flowering hedges that defined the road were giving way to clusters of small houses, each with its own garden, and at the bottom of the sloping high street she could see the bobbing masts of the yachts in the harbour.

The small town of Port Serrat clung to the hills around the harbour. It was a quaint place, much of it very old, and she remembered Ryan used to entertain the tourists with tales of its disreputable past. In the eighteenth and nineteenth centuries, it had been a haunt for pirates and buccaneers, and according to him they accounted for the number of bars and inns that thronged its streets.

Megan parked the buggy in a chandler's yard, and then sauntered down towards the quay. A fish market occupied one corner of the quayside, with every kind of seafood imaginable. There were shrimps and crabs, and wriggling lobsters, and shark and salmon and grouper. Many of the varieties of fish Megan hadn't tasted since she was last here, and she guessed Anita had no problem in varying the menu.

Beyond the fish market, the quay opened out into a marina, where the tall-masted vessels she had seen as she'd driven into town jostled prettily on their moorings. Like Barbados and Antigua, San Felipe attracted sea-going yachts, but many of these vessels were privately owned or charters.

Ryan used to own a yacht, she remembered, which was

how her parents had got to know him so well. He used to enjoy ferrying his guests around the island, or on longer expeditions to other islands in the group.

She was beginning to feel thirsty, and, finding a small café, she seated herself outside, beneath a huge striped umbrella. When the waiter appeared, she ordered a glass of sweet lemonade, and sat there, sipping the ice-cold liquid with genuine enjoyment.

Glancing at her watch, she discovered it was only a little after half-past ten. She'd left the hotel early, to make the most of the less oppressive heat of the morning, and now she was very glad she had. She had lots of time to do a little window-shopping before visiting the cemetery Anita had described to her, and then she'd drive back to the hotel for lunch.

When she left the café, she couldn't help wondering where Remy's flat was situated. He'd said he lived near the harbour, but there were no obvious pointers as to whereabouts. There were no modern apartment blocks here, just a wealth of colourful housing, and she guessed his home was hidden amongst them.

Of course, his office was something else, she reflected, glad she had kept her hat on as she slogged up the busy main street. This area of town was famous for its shops and boutiques catering for the rich tourist market, and her eyes were drawn to the colourful displays of designer goods.

It was possible he worked at home, she mused, but she didn't think that was likely. A lawyer would need to be accessible to his clients, and she thought Remy would want to keep his public and private lives separate.

And then she saw him. He was several yards ahead of her, walking with another man, and she thought it said something about her state of mind that she recognised him at once. Even from behind, his broad shoulders and lean, muscled thighs were unmistakable. He moved with such a lithe, easy grace, his identity was not in any doubt to her.

But what should she do? Despite the fact that he wasn't wearing a jacket today, his shirt and trousers were formal, evidence surely that he was working. Besides, the last thing she wanted was for him to think she was looking for him. However innocent her curiosity, she'd rather keep it to herself.

She halted uncertainly, glancing back towards the harbour, but when she looked round again she found he and his companion had halted, too. Remy appeared to be saying goodbye to the other man, his hand raised to push open a nearby door. Was that where he had his office? she wondered. Over one of the shops that lined the street?

And then he saw her.

Despite the hat, despite the incongruity of finding her here, in Port Serrat, alone, his recognition of her was just as immediate. Before she could move, before she could turn and hurry down the street and pretend she hadn't recognised him, he bid his companion farewell and came striding towards her, and Megan could only stand and wait for him, her stomach quivering in anticipation.

CHAPTER SEVEN

To HER relief, he seemed pleased to see her. She'd been rather apprehensive that after their previous conversation he might be holding a grudge. But she should have known better, she admitted. She wasn't that important to him.

'How did you get here?' he asked now, by way of a greeting, and Megan wondered if he thought she'd come with his mother. His mobile mouth tilted. 'Nice hat!'

'Yes, isn't it?' Megan tugged the brim around her cheeks and pulled a face at him. 'And, believe it or not, I came by buggy.' She nodded up the street. 'Is that where you work?'

'Alone?'

Megan frowned, pretending to misunderstand him. 'Yes, I know. You told me you worked alone.'

'No, I mean—' Remy started to explain, and then caught her smiling. 'You knew what I meant,' he accused good-naturedly. 'I thought Mom might have brought you. Are you supposed to drive?'

'I do have a licence,' she declared sweetly, enjoying their exchange much more than she should. She sobered. 'And it is almost six weeks since I had the operation. I'm feeling pretty good, as a matter of fact.'

'Yes, I can see that.' Remy's eyes made a disturbing résumé of her slender figure, lingering longest on her bare legs. 'And as you are here—and alone—perhaps we could have lunch together?'

'Well...'

Megan's tone mirrored her hesitation and Remy was quick to give her an escape. 'Of course, you've probably got other things to do,' he said. 'I'm sorry. I wasn't thinking. Perhaps you want to get back to the hotel and rest.'

'Oh, please!' Megan couldn't let him think that. 'Apart from visiting the cemetery, I've got nothing planned.'

'So?'

'So—yes. I would like to have lunch with you.' She paused. 'Where shall we meet? You know this place much better than me.'

Remy considered. 'Why not come back here, and I'll show you round the office?' he suggested. He gestured towards a sports shop set further up the street. 'Use the side door and come straight up.'

'All right.'

Megan beamed, and Remy stared at her for a moment before turning away. Then, as she was heading back down the street, he hailed her. 'I'm glad you came,' he called, and she hugged the words to herself all the way back to the car.

The Baptist cemetery, where Laura Robards' ashes had been scattered, was on the outskirts of the small town. It was set on the cliffs, overlooking the harbour, and Megan guessed Ryan must have come here often before his illness had confined him to the hotel. Within the Garden of Remembrance she found a small plaque with her mother's name engraved on it, and the words 'I Miss You' half hidden behind an enormous vase of orchids and lilies.

It was immensely poignant and immensely moving. Megan was alone in the garden, and she groped blindly for the stone bench that allowed visitors to sit for a while and share the garden's peace. And after a while a little of that peace crept over her, too, assuring her of her mother's forgiveness, and giving her a sense of completion.

It was after twelve when she walked up the high street again, and despite what she had said to Remy earlier, she was beginning to feel weary. After all, she'd only taken fairly undemanding walks since her illness, and although she had felt all right when she'd accepted his invitation now she half wished she'd headed straight back to the hotel.

She pushed open the glass door to one side of the sports shop he had indicated, noticing the name outlined on the glass beneath her hand. 'Jeremy Robards,' she read. 'Attorney at Law.' Funny, she reflected ruefully, she'd never realised that Remy wasn't his full name.

The stairs were steep, and by the time she got to the top she was panting. She stood for a moment on the landing, trying to get her breath before entering the office, and then started in surprise when the door was opened and a young black woman emerged.

She was a pretty woman, small and rather voluptuous, and her eyes were kind and they immediately darkened with concern. 'Are you all right?' she exclaimed, slipping an arm about Megan's waist and leading her back into the office. 'Do you feel faint? Would you like a glass of water? Let me tell Remy you're here.'

'No, really—' began Megan, sinking down weakly onto the worn leather sofa that ran along one wall of what she now realised was a kind of waiting room. Across the room, a desk occupied by a word processor seemed to indicate a secretary, though at the moment there was no one else about. 'I'll be fine.'

The young woman ignored her, hurrying across the rubber-tiled floor to an inner door. She tapped once and then opened it with the familiarity of long usage, and Megan realised she must work here, too.

For herself, Megan wished the floor would open up and swallow her. She had never felt so helpless in her life. Except maybe the afternoon when her ulcer had perforated, she acknowledged. And at least she wasn't in pain at the moment.

Her head was buzzing, and she had no idea what the woman said to Remy. But presently he was there, squatting down in front of her, his expression full of the kind of sympathy she couldn't cope with. 'Dammit, Megan,' he said, sweeping off her hat, 'what the hell have you been doing to yourself now?'

Megan drew a breath. 'Your stairs are steep, that's all.'

'Oh, right. And that's why you're as pale as a ghost.'

'I'm tired,' she defended herself. 'Perhaps I've tried to

do too much. I'll be all right as soon as I get my breath back.'

'Will you?' Remy didn't sound convinced, though he got abruptly to his feet. 'A glass of water, please, Sylvie,' he requested politely. 'Then you can leave Miss Cross to me.'

Sylvie got the water, smiling sympathetically, and Megan drank thirstily from the glass. Perhaps she was just dehydrated, she thought. That was why she felt so wobbly. But her legs were still like jelly when she got to her feet.

'Where are you going?' Sylvie had departed after delivering the water, and now Remy stepped between her and the door.

'I thought we were going for lunch,' protested Megan, making a vain attempt to appear enthusiastic. 'Oh, yes.' She remembered. 'You were going to show me your office.'

Remy's nostrils flared. 'You don't seriously expect me to take you to a restaurant when you're shaking like a leaf.'

'I'm not shaking.' But she was. 'Oh, I'll be all right in a few minutes. It was hot up at the cemetery, and I suppose I'm not used to hill-walking.'

Remy's mouth compressed. 'All right,' he said, and she was surprised at how easily he had given in. 'We'll have lunch. But not at a restaurant.' Which explained his compliance. 'My apartment's not far from here. We'll eat there.'

Megan's mouth rounded to make an objection, but the warning look in his eyes deterred her. Why not? she thought, pushing aside the suspicion that it really wasn't a good idea to go to his home. She had been dreading the possibility of making a fool of herself in public. And what was she afraid of, after all? She had been curious to see where he lived.

Lifting her shoulders in a gesture of acceptance, she followed Remy across the room and into his office. A square sun-lit room, with long windows overlooking the harbour, it was much more attractive than her own office at home. She would swop her steel and chrome technology for a view like that, she thought enviously, and Remy's ancient

mahogany desk and leather chair matched their antique surroundings.

'This is where you work?' she murmured, observing the
bulging filing cabinets and the desk that was loaded down
with briefs.

'When I have the time,' he answered, shoving his wallet
into his pocket. 'That's it. I'm ready.' He glanced around
with some resignation. 'I've got a court appearance this
afternoon so I've got to be back by two.'

'Oh.'

Megan wondered if he was regretting offering the invitation as much as she was regretting accepting it, but she
met his eyes and decided not to ask. She had the feeling
her appearance had caused enough aggravation as it was.

It was easier going down the stairs, though Megan clung
to the handrail, just in case. She'd snatched up her hat again
before leaving, and now she tugged it back onto her head,
uncaring of what Remy might think.

Outside, the midday heat was enervating. Megan felt herself wilting, and hoped Remy's apartment wasn't far away.
She didn't object either when he gripped her arm just above
her elbow to guide her, though the feeling of those hard
fingers against her flesh was far too disturbing.

'It's not far,' he said, his voice only marginally less
clipped than before, and Megan forced a grateful smile.

'What a state to be in,' she said. 'Falling apart just because I've done a bit of sightseeing. You must think I'm a
complete idiot.'

'What I think is best not stated,' retorted Remy shortly,
matching his steps to hers. 'I should have gone to the cemetery with you. Or my mother should, anyway. It was too
long a journey to make alone.'

'That's not true.' Megan couldn't allow him to think that.
She bit her lip. 'And your mother did offer to come with
me, as a matter of fact. But I wanted to come on my own.'

'Why?'

They had turned down a side street, where the jutting
balconies of old buildings provided a blessed escape from

the sun, and before Megan could think of an answer Remy
had paused beside a narrow opening. A brick passageway
led into a kind of inner courtyard, and he ushered Megan
ahead of him into the square beyond.

'Welcome to Moonraker's Yard,' he announced drily,
glancing about him. 'I'm afraid you're going to have to
climb a few more stairs.'

Megan shook her head, too bemused by the charm of her
surroundings to worry about something as ordinary as
stairs. They were in a kind of mews, with the sun beating
down upon their heads from between a circle of tall houses,
with narrow wooden steps giving access to the floors above.

'This is where you live?' she asked, and Remy nodded.
'It's not as decrepit inside as it appears.'

'Oh, no.' Megan was vehement. 'It doesn't look decrepit
at all. I was just thinking how delightful it was.'

'You're obviously a romantic,' said Remy, with a wry
grimace. 'Come on. My pad's just up here.'

They climbed one of the flights of wooden stairs to a
studded wooden door, and after Remy had used his key
they stepped into a long corridor. At the end of the corridor,
light flooded from a stained-glass window, covering the
floor with prisms of light in a hundred different colours and
shades.

'Oh!'

Megan barely had a chance to exclaim at the unusual
design of the window before Remy had closed the door and
was striding away to open a door on their right. 'Come in,'
he said, gesturing for her to follow him, and she moved
almost dreamily into a room that seemed both ancient and
modern.

It was obviously his living room, and although it was
fairly large the low ceiling, with its dark oak beams, gave
it a cosy appearance. The walls, two of which were panelled
and gleamed with the patina of age, were hung with several
impressive oil paintings, and a huge urn of flowers filled
the wide stone hearth.

The furniture was eclectic: wide squashy sofas existing

cheek-by-jowl with cabinets from another age. There were Victorian bookshelves, and an eighteenth-century captain's table, and various tubs and planters filled with climbing plants.

The windows were long and narrow, like the hall, but the view was expansive. From here, it was possible to see the whole sweep of the harbour and the bay. One of the windows was ajar, and a slight breeze moved the long curtains—curtains which were almost transparent, and reflected the colours of the sea.

Megan drew a trembling breath and gazed all about her. 'It's fantastic,' she said. 'I never expected anything like this.'

'What did you expect?' he enquired lightly, tilting back the brim of her hat. 'That I probably lived in a loft somewhere, without any running water?'

'Well, no.' She moistened her lips. 'But this is so—so—'

'Rustic?'

'Tasteful,' she insisted firmly. She lifted her shoulders. 'You're very lucky to live in a place like this.'

'Am I?'

His tone was sardonic, but Megan chose not to answer him, approaching the windows instead, and resting one knee on the low sill. 'What a marvellous view!' she exclaimed. 'You must never tire of looking at it. I bet it's pretty at night when all the lights are lit.'

'You'll have to come and see for yourself,' remarked Remy evenly, opening a door at the far side of the room. 'Will cheese and salad do? I'm afraid I don't have anything more sophisticated. I wasn't expecting to have a guest for lunch.'

'Of course.' Megan felt guilty. 'Please—don't put yourself out for me. Anything will do—a sandwich or some fruit, even. I'm really not very hungry at all.'

Remy pulled a face and disappeared though the door, and after depositing her hat on one of the winged armchairs Megan followed him. She found herself in a small kitchen which was surprisingly well equipped, with pans and bunches of herbs hanging from the beams. There was a dresser lined with dishes in a cream and gold design, and a tiny window looking out onto a terrace.

Remy was in the process of taking a dish of crisp lettuce from the fridge, along with some of the tiny cherry tomatoes that Megan knew were so sweet. A loaf of crusty French bread rested on a wooden board, beside a huge chunk of cheese and a dish of creamy butter.

'You're supposed to be taking it easy,' he declared at once when he saw her, and she pulled a face.

'I feel much better now,' she insisted, and she did. The thick walls of the old building kept the apartment delightfully cool, and although she still felt a little flushed she had stopped shaking.

'Well, why don't you go and sit at the table?' he suggested, gesturing towards an archway she hadn't noticed before. Beyond the fronds of greenery that hung from the ceiling she now saw a tiny dining area, with a square mahogany table and four ladder-backed chairs. 'Here—' he handed her two place mats and some cutlery '—take these with you. And there are some glasses in the cabinet right behind you. I know you don't want anything alcoholic, but I've got some mineral water in the fridge.'

Megan laid the table, and then did as he suggested and sat by the window, which, like the living room, looked out over the harbour. She might be feeling a little guilty, not having let Anita know what she was doing, but if she was honest she would admit that she had seldom felt so happy in her life.

The food, when it came, was simple and delicious. As well as the lettuce and tomatoes, there were tangy radishes and sweet peppers and thin slices of cucumber. The bread was cut into crusty chunks, which she spread with some of the yellow butter, and the cheese was ripe and crumbly, and full of flavour.

'So,' said Remy, circling the rim of his glass with a lazy finger, 'why did you want to come alone? Is Mom getting on your nerves already?'

'No!' But Megan wondered at his perception. 'Your mother and I get along—very well.' She paused. 'I just wanted a little time on my own, that's all.'

'So what are you doing here?' he countered, and she coloured.

'Well—this wasn't planned to happen.'

'Wasn't it?'

'No.' She forced herself to meet his knowing gaze. 'It wasn't. But that doesn't mean I'm not glad it did.'

His eyes darkened. 'Good.'

Megan drew a trembling breath. 'Anyway, I doubt your mother would approve.'

He didn't argue. 'No.'

'I think she's afraid I'll be a bad influence on you,' added Megan, attempting to lighten the mood. 'I'm not sure she entirely approves of me. Not being married and so on.'

'You could be right.' He smiled. 'And you like the apartment?'

'Mmm.' Megan nodded, taking a sip of iced water before replying. 'What I've seen of it anyway,' she said. She moistened her lips. 'Will—will you and Rachel live here after you're married?'

Remy's tawny eyes darkened. 'Who says we're getting married?'

Megan shrugged. 'Well, aren't you?'

'Not to my knowledge,' he retorted shortly. 'When are you marrying Simon?'

'I'm not. That is—' Megan looked down at her plate. 'It's not something we've ever discussed.' Which was true, she told herself defensively, though perhaps not for any reason Remy might assume. 'We're friends, that's all. And—and business partners.'

Remy moved his broad shoulders. 'Well, so are Rachel and I—friends, at least. As she doesn't have a job, we could hardly be business partners.'

Megan pressed her lips together and then, lifting her head, she looked him squarely in the eye. 'That's not exactly true, is it?'

Remy's stare was daunting. 'Isn't it?'

'No.' Megan hesitated. 'I've assumed that Rachel and you—well, that you're lovers,' she said hurriedly. 'Friends don't usually sleep together.'

Remy gave a snort. 'Don't they?' His tone was disparaging. 'You sound like my mother.'

Megan endeavoured not to show any reaction, but his words stung. 'Well, I suppose I am your aunt—your *step*-aunt, at least,' she reminded him crisply. 'I didn't think you'd mind me showing some interest in your future. I didn't mean to pry.'

'Didn't you?' Remy, who had eaten very little, she noticed, pushed his plate aside and got abruptly to his feet. 'I think you were being honest for once, and now you're trying to rationalise it. Don't pretend you feel like my aunt, because I don't believe it. You're concerned because you're becoming attracted to me, and you know your father would never have approved.'

'No!' Megan was horrified.

'Yes.' Remy came round the table and pulled her roughly to her feet. His hands massaged her shoulders. 'That's why you came looking for me today. Because we never have any privacy at the hotel.'

'You're wrong—'

'Am I?' Patently, he didn't believe her, and she could hardly blame him when her insides were churning and her heart was thudding erratically in her chest. He bent his head and rubbed his mouth against hers in a light, taunting caress. 'Stop kidding yourself, Megan. You might not like it, but you knew what was happening that first evening when you spilled your drink.'

'That's not true.' Despite the fact that the brush of his lips had started a fire that spread wantonly throughout her body, Megan fought to be free of him. She could not allow him to think she had come here with some wild notion of starting an affair. Until he'd accused her of being attracted to him, she'd thought she'd done a good job of hiding her emotions. To discover her feelings were so transparent was humiliating, apart from creating a situation she couldn't deal with. 'Will you let go of me?'

Remy held her for a few seconds longer, his breath cool against her hot forehead. Then he spread his fingers wide, enabling her to move out from under their restraint, and she stumbled back instinctively, putting the width of her chair between them. But she could tell from his expression that he still didn't believe her; that he had only let her go because he'd chosen to do so.

Megan was breathing rapidly. Where before she had regarded the confines of the dining room as cosily intimate, now she was only conscious of its limited space. To get out of the room she was forced to squeeze past him, and it didn't help to know that her embarrassment was as evident as her indignation.

She hurried through the kitchen, pausing on the threshold to the living room because she found her head was spinning. Oh, God, she thought, she surely wasn't going to make a fool of herself again. She had to remember she was still convalescing and not go charging about as if she were fit and well.

'What are you doing?'

Remy was behind her now, his voice low and full of resignation. But when she would have moved away his hand at her waist prevented her, sliding beneath the loosened hem of her shirt and stroking her skin.

'What do you think you're doing?' she countered, stiffening automatically away from him. She took a breath. 'I'm leaving. Thank you for lunch. It was—well, it was—interesting.'

'Megan—'

'What?' Unable to bear the caress of his cool fingers or the heat of his body behind her, she swung away from him then, feeling her balance tilt and then right itself as the dizziness attacked her again. 'Look, Remy, I'm sorry if I've given you the wrong impression. I was curious about where you lived and worked, I'll admit it. But anything else is purely in your head.'

'Really?'

'Yes, really.' She looked about for her hat. However much she wanted to get out of here, she dared not go without it.

'Okay.' Remy's sigh was weary. 'If that's how you want to play it.'

'Play it?' Megan found her hat and jammed it onto her head with a shaking hand. 'I don't know what you're talking about. I'm not playing. I like you, Remy. I like you a lot. But I can't see you as anything more than the boy I used to play with.'

'Bullshit.'

Megan caught her breath. 'I beg your pardon?'

'I said—'

'I know what you said, but you had no right to say it.' She swallowed. 'I'm sorry if you don't believe me, but that's the way it is.'

'I don't believe you.' He was scathing. 'You've just had second thoughts, that's all.'

'No.' Megan couldn't believe she was having this conversation with him. 'Please—you know your mother would be so upset if she knew what was going on—'

'My mother!' Remy said the words almost contemptuously. 'Of course. We mustn't forget my mother's part in all this, must we? What's wrong? Are you afraid we're going to offend her? My God, it's been a long time since I allowed my mother to make any decisions in my life.'

Megan moved her head from side to side. 'Remy—'

'What?'

She edged towards the door. 'This is crazy.'

'I agree.' But instead of abandoning the argument he closed the space between them. Cupping her hot face between his palms, he looked down at her with dark intent. 'Don't you get it, Megan? I don't care why you came here as long as you stay.'

Megan's lips parted. 'I can't.'

'Why can't you?' His fingertips probed the soft contours of her ears. 'This isn't anything to do with anyone else. It's to do with us, that's all. With the fact that you want me as much as I want you.'

'No!'

Megan would have moved away from him then, but the closed door was at her back and there was no place to go. Her mouth was dry, but when his thumb rubbed sensuously across her lower lip she felt wet in other places. He was playing with her emotions, she thought, in a panic, and there was nothing she could do to stop him.

She couldn't believe this was happening. Any minute now Remy would let her go and admit that he'd just been teasing her. But deep inside her she knew it was no game. Remy was actually preventing her from leaving.

And, to add to her distress, she knew that everything he'd said was true. She didn't understand all of it, but she couldn't deny that she was attracted to him, and beneath his hands the blood was rushing hotly to the surface of her skin. She wanted him to touch her; dammit, she wanted to touch him, and rivulets of fire seemed to be attacking every nerve in her body.

He was removing her hat now, bending his head to stroke the sensitive skin behind her ear with his tongue. She felt weak, and she tried to tell herself it was a hangover from her illness, but when he wedged his knee between her thighs she was more concerned he'd feel the dampness between her legs.

'You're trembling again,' he said huskily, his anger dissipating at the knowledge of her vulnerability, and she wondered if he'd believe her if she pretended she was going to faint. But then his mouth moved across her cheek and found her parted lips, and such strategies were no longer an option.

CHAPTER EIGHT

ALTHOUGH it was the last thing she would have chosen to face, Megan wasn't really surprised to find Anita waiting for her when she got back.

'Oh, so there you are!' Anita exclaimed, when Megan had parked the buggy outside the hotel. 'I was beginning to get anxious. You didn't tell me you intended to have lunch in town.'

'It—was a spur-of-the-moment thing,' began Megan, wondering if Remy could have phoned his mother and told her she'd been to his apartment, but before she could incriminate herself Anita made it plain that he hadn't.

'I've been trying to get in touch with Remy,' she declared. 'I wondered if you might have called at his office. But Sylvie—that's his secretary, you know—she said he'd gone out with a client at twelve o'clock and hadn't come back.'

A client!

Megan wondered if that was Sylvie's interpretation of who she was or Remy's. She had the feeling it was the former. From the little she had seen of her, Sylvie had appeared to be a very shrewd assistant.

'So did you go to the cemetery?' asked Anita, inadvertently letting Megan off the hook. And at her stepsister's nod she said, 'It's a pretty place, isn't it? Pops used to spend hours sitting in the garden.'

'I guessed as much,' Megan murmured. 'I sat there for a while, too.'

'Did you?' Anita hooked her arm through hers and led her into the hotel. Then she gave Megan a thoughtful stare. 'You look tired. Are you sure you haven't done too much?'

'Of course not.' But Megan could feel her colour rising

in spite of her efforts. 'I am a little tired, though. You're right about that. If you don't mind, I'll have a rest before dinner.'

'You don't feel up to visiting with Pops, I suppose?' Anita ventured hopefully. 'He asked for you this morning, and I had to tell him you'd gone into town.'

Megan gave an inward groan, but she turned to Anita with a determined smile. 'Why not?' she said. 'I'd like to tell him where I've been.'

'Thank you.'

Anita squeezed her arm and then let her go, and Megan restored her hat before stepping outside again. Although it was after three o'clock, the sun was still as hot as ever, and the wide brim gave some protection to her eyes as well.

It only took a few minutes to reach Ryan's bungalow. It was the one furthest from the beach and therefore in the quietest position. As always, the nurse on duty was pleased to see her. It enabled him to relax for a few minutes, knowing his patient was not alone.

Ryan appeared to be asleep, but Megan had learned not to be deceived. During the course of their many conversations, he had told her that he seldom slept for long, day or night. He closed his eyes and dozed sometimes, but he never got what she would have called a good night's sleep.

'You're back,' he said as she approached the bed, pulling off the oxygen mask so that he could speak. His voice was harsh and often laboured, but she'd got used to that, too. She no longer felt like running for assistance if he appeared to be short of breath.

'Yes,' she said now, sinking down into the chair the nurse had placed beside the bed for her. 'How are you?'

'What is it they say? As well as can be expected,' he muttered humorously. 'Did you enjoy your outing? Anita said you might be going to the cemetery.'

'Yes. I did.' Megan nodded, looking at his thin wrist which lay beside hers on the sheet. 'It's a very peaceful spot, isn't it? I think it did me good.'

'Good, good.' He echoed the word, his lips twitching

involuntarily at his own thoughts. 'Laura and I used to spend a lot of time together, when I could still walk from the car to the bench.'

Megan pressed her lips together. 'I'm sure she misses your visits,' she said, before caution could silence her tongue. 'That is—I think it's where she'd have wanted to rest.'

'Do you?' His eyes bored into hers. And then, as if what he wanted to say required some effort, he pressed the mask briefly to his face. 'You don't know how grateful I am to hear you say that, Meggie.' His hand groped for hers. 'Does that mean you've forgiven me at last?'

Megan breathed deeply, allowing him to enfold her soft fingers within his dry flesh. 'I suppose it does.'

'Thank you.' He sighed. 'You've made me very happy. Remy said you didn't bear grudges and he was right.'

Remy...

Megan would have preferred not to think about Remy at that moment. Indeed, she'd been trying to stop thinking about him ever since she'd left Moonraker's Yard. Not that she'd done anything wrong, she assured herself firmly. She had nothing to be ashamed of, and she should stop blaming herself for his mistakes.

'You like my boy, don't you?' the old man continued now, and Megan attempted not to betray her fears.

'We're—old friends,' she said, wanting to withdraw her hand before he sensed her apprehension. She licked her lips. 'I'm not tiring you, am I?'

'I'll survive,' he said sardonically. 'For the present anyway.' His lips twisted. 'Tell me what you think about him. His mother's proud because he's become a lawyer.'

'And you're not?' The words slipped past Megan's lips once again, and hot colour bathed her cheeks at her audacity.

'Of course I'm proud of him,' Ryan said unevenly, resorting to the oxygen mask once more. 'But Remy knows where his real loyalties lie. The hotel will eventually be his responsibility.' He coughed. 'He knows that as well as me.'

Megan absorbed his words, realising that he regarded Remy's career as nothing more than a stop-gap, a way to fill his time until he was needed. She could see that in his way Ryan was as single-minded as her father had been. They both believed they knew what was best for their children.

'I'll have to be going,' she said, hoping to avoid an answer, but Ryan's fingers tightened round her hand for a moment.

'Has he told you?' he asked succinctly. 'Has he told you about his father?' He swallowed with some difficulty. 'If he hasn't, it's important that he should.'

'Told me what?' Megan was confused. She'd assumed that was a topic that was never broached.

'Your father never told you?' he wheezed, clearly getting agitated. 'Why would he? He despised us for it.'

'Mr Robards—'

'Ryan.'

'Ryan, then.' Megan paused. 'I'm afraid I don't know what you're talking about.'

'No.' Another harsh cough tore through his narrow frame, and this time he had to release her hand to grope for the box of tissues lying on the bed beside him. 'I'm sorry,' he said when he was able, obviously tiring. 'We'll have to discuss this at some other time.'

'Of course.'

Megan got to her feet at once, hoping that Ryan would have forgotten this conversation the next time she came. Anita had told her that he was inclined to be forgetful, the drugs he was being given for the cancer acting as a sedative as well.

It was good to be outside again, but for once she didn't hurry back to the hotel. Her mind was buzzing with thoughts of what he might have been trying to tell her, and she wondered why he thought Remy's parentage would mean anything to her.

It wasn't as if she had any lasting role to play in his life. Despite what had almost happened that afternoon, their relationship to one another was unlikely to change. And she didn't want it to, she told herself, even if she was attracted to him.

Reaching the foyer, she crossed to the lifts and, finding one vacant, stepped inside and pressed the button for the penthouse floor. Leaning against the fabric-covered wall, she felt an overwhelming sense of relief that she hadn't done something foolish when she was with Remy. If she'd submitted to her baser instincts, how could she have faced Anita again?

Once inside her room, she shed her hat and shoes and padded wearily into the bathroom. Turning on the shower, she stripped off the rest of her clothes and then stepped under the cooling spray. Tilting back her head, she let the fall of water revive her for a few moments, before reaching for her favourite brand of soap.

However, although the shower was supposed to rid her mind of thoughts of Remy, and the sinful pleasures thinking of him evoked, she found the simple task of cleansing herself inspired images she couldn't ignore. As she soaped her breasts, she couldn't help but remember the way Remy had held her, how his hands had slid up beneath her shirt and found the taut nipples that had surged against his palms...

She took a deep breath, trying not to recall the hungry passion of his kiss. But once the idea was seeded it couldn't help but take root, and she sank against the tiled wall of the cubicle, shaking uncontrollably.

It shouldn't have happened, she told herself. She shouldn't have gone to Remy's office, and she most definitely shouldn't have gone to his apartment. It was all very well telling herself that she had had no hidden motives for accepting his invitation, but if she was brutally honest she'd admit that she hadn't been entirely impartial either.

So what had she expected? she asked herself. It was too easy to excuse her behaviour on the grounds that she hadn't had a lot of choice in the matter. In actual fact, as soon as she'd felt unwell, she should have headed straight back to the hotel.

Whether Remy would have allowed her to do that was another matter, of course, and the fact that she hadn't felt ill until she'd reached his office would have complicated the situation, she supposed. But she was pretty sure he wouldn't have propositioned her if she'd kept him at a distance. It had been stupid to ask him all those personal questions. He must have thought she was checking out the competition.

A shudder of revulsion swept over her, and, pushing herself away from the wall, she started to soap her legs. It wasn't the first time she'd felt the need to get things into perspective, but she hadn't realised she was quite so transparent before.

His accusation had caught her completely unawares. She wasn't used to men—or women, for that matter—who voiced their feelings so openly. It wasn't just that he was good-looking; she'd known good-looking men before. It was something about him personally that had such a devastating effect on her hormones.

Yet there'd been something vaguely scornful about the way he'd challenged her. Almost as if he'd despised her for the very feelings he'd attempted to expose. Perhaps he thought she'd come on to him to liven up her holiday, and whatever she might regret about that afternoon he had certainly done that.

Her breathing quickened. Soaping her legs had reminded her of how reckless she had been. When he'd pushed his thigh between her thighs and chafed that most sensitive part of her anatomy, she'd almost lost control. It would have been so easy to give in to him, so easy to ignore the outcome at that moment. For the first time in her life, she'd discovered what it was like to actually want a man. And she'd wanted him so badly, she'd been dizzy at the thought.

But somehow she hadn't given in. Despite the fact that the sensual heat of his mouth had burned her senses, she'd clung onto her sanity. Perhaps her swimming head had been her saviour; perhaps the groan she'd uttered had pierced his sensual haze. Whatever, he'd let her escape from him, and she hadn't waited to find out what he really thought.

She remembered that walk back to where she'd left the buggy only vaguely, but she did remember how relieved she'd been to find it was still there. Even the scorching leather of the seats had been preferable to the anguish she was feeling, and she'd driven away from Port Serrat with no intention of ever going back.

She was half afraid Remy might appear at dinner. She wasn't at all sure what she'd do if she found him waiting for her in his mother's sitting room, but to her relief she didn't have to find out. Only Anita was there, scanning a sheaf of bills the office manager had given her, but she thrust the papers aside when Megan came into the room.

'How are you feeling now?' Anita asked, ever the courteous hostess, and Megan knew a moment's irritation at the enquiry.

'Much better,' she answered, remembering Anita hadn't shown such concern for her earlier. 'Thank you.'

'Good.' Anita paused, and then, as if her thoughts had moved onto the same wavelength, she asked, 'Did you spend long with my father?'

'Not long.' Megan was noncommittal, accepting the other woman's mimed offer of a mineral water with a nod. 'He seemed pleased that I'd been to the cemetery.'

'I'm sure he would be.' Anita handed her a glass. 'It's good you could share that with him.'

'Yes.' Megan took a tentative sip of her drink. 'Mmm, this is lovely.'

'Did he talk about your mother at all?'

Clearly Anita wanted to know everything, and it was true that Megan had suffered several of these debriefings after spending time with Ryan. 'He wanted me to forgive him,' she said quietly. 'I think it's been preying on his mind. I think we've made our peace with one another at last.'

'I'm glad.' Anita resumed her seat. 'I suppose you realise that's why he wanted to see you.'

Megan hesitated. 'Remy hinted as much,' she said at last, taking the bull by the horns, and Anita frowned.

'He did?' she asked tersely. 'I don't think it was his place to tell you anything. I must have a word with him the next time I see him.'

'Oh, no—' Megan broke off, wishing she hadn't been so indiscreet. 'That is, he thought I knew,' she offered lamely. 'And of course you didn't know he knew how ill his grand-father is.'

Anita frowned again. 'You didn't tell Pops that Remy had said—'

'No. Oh, no.' Megan was adamant. 'We hardly mentioned Remy at all.'

Anita's eyes narrowed. 'But you did speak of him?'

'A little.' Megan felt as if she was getting into deeper and deeper water.

'In what connection?' Clearly, Anita saw nothing wrong in being so inquisitive. 'I suppose he complained about the hotel.'

'About the hotel?' Megan shook her head in confusion. 'I don't think he complained about the hotel.'

'But I assume he told you he expects Remy to take over when—when it's necessary.' Anita nodded. 'That is one of his hang-ups, I'm afraid.'

Megan said nothing, afraid to voice an opinion in case she was wrong. 'I wonder what we're having for dinner?' she ventured instead, hoping to change the subject, but Anita fixed her with a calculating gaze.

'You didn't suggest that Remy should be allowed to lead his own life, did you?' she persisted. 'When I saw Pops earlier this evening, he seemed a bit restless to me. I thought at first it was because he'd had a bad day, but it wasn't so. According to his nurse, he was all right before your visit.'

Megan's jaw sagged. 'Do you think that I—'

'I don't think anything,' said Anita hurriedly. 'But as you'd been discussing Remy...'

'We hadn't been discussing Remy.' Megan was indignant.

'So what were you talking about?'

'This and that.'

'So what did he say?'

'Who?' Megan was confused. 'Remy?' Which she realised said more about her train of thought than Anita's.

'No, not Remy,' said her stepsister shortly. 'You haven't been talking to Remy, have you? I meant what did my father say about my son?'

Megan was glad of the shadows in the room which hid her expression. She'd already regretted not being honest with Anita—about meeting Remy, at least—and now she felt as if she'd been snagged on the horns of her own dilemma. It suddenly occurred to her that Anita might mention Megan's outing to her son, and he might admit quite openly that he'd seen her.

Oh, God!

It seemed the lesser evil to be frank about this situation anyway and, after taking a drink, she viewed her stepsister warily over the glass. 'Your father asked if Remy had told me about—about his father,' she said, somewhat defiantly. 'I don't know why. It's nothing to do with me.'

'No, it's not.'

Clearly, Anita was irritated now, and Megan guessed she didn't like the idea of her father discussing family business with a virtual stranger.

'Well, he hasn't,' Megan offered, hoping to placate her. 'Remy hasn't spoken about his father at all.' She bit her lip. 'It's not something we'd talk about.' She hesitated. 'I imagine it's as painful to him as it obviously is to you.'

'Why should you assume that talking about Remy's father would be painful to me?' Anita countered. She sucked in a breath. 'What else has my father said?'

'Nothing.' Megan gave an inward groan. 'Honestly, nothing. I wish I'd never mentioned it.'

Anita regarded her narrowly. 'Did your own father talk to you about me?' she asked suddenly.

'No.' Megan was defensive. 'We never talked about you or Remy after—after the divorce.'

'You're sure about that?'

'Of course I'm sure.' Megan was feeling indignant again now. 'If you're ashamed of how it happened, as I said before, it's nothing to do with me.'

'Ashamed!' Anita looked horrified, and despite her own resentment Megan wanted to curl up and die at the look on Anita's face. It wasn't her nature to upset anyone, and particularly not someone who had been kind to her.

'You really don't understand, do you?' Anita exclaimed wonderingly. 'For all you said your father hadn't said anything, I couldn't believe you didn't know the truth.' She waved a dismissive hand at the waiter who had appeared in the doorway. 'Later,' she said firmly, leaving him in no doubt as to who was in charge here. And then, to Megan, she said, 'Obviously he never discussed my mother with you either.'

'Your mother?' Megan shook her head. 'No. Why would he?'

'Because she was the reason Daddy moved to San Felipe in the first place.' Anita paused. 'My mother was black, Megan. And people weren't as—enlightened in the fifties as they are today.'

CHAPTER NINE

MEGAN was stunned. Of all the things she might have expected Anita to say, she had never thought of anything like this. And yet, when she thought of it, it made a cruel kind of sense. But it was her first brush, however distant, with racism, and she didn't like the ugly images it had inspired.

'I've shocked you, haven't I?' Anita's tone was flat, and Megan realised how her silence must seem to her stepsister. 'But perhaps now you can appreciate why your father was so antagonistic towards me and towards Remy.'

'No!' Megan was appalled, but not because she sympathised with her father's prejudiced views. And then, because even now her tongue was inclined to act independently of her brain, she said, 'But you look—you look so—'

'White?' Anita got up from her chair and moved towards the open windows, tilting her head to gaze up at the arc of black velvet above. 'Or sufficiently so to pass as white on an island like San Felipe?' she queried. She turned towards Megan again. 'I don't know whether that's a compliment or not.'

'It wasn't meant to be a compliment!' Megan exclaimed forcefully. 'But, Lord, Anita, you can't drop something like that into the conversation and not expect me to react.' She shook her head. 'I'm sorry if I'm being clumsy. What I meant was, I never would have guessed.'

'No.' Anita's smile was sardonic. 'You and Remy's father both.' She took a deep breath. 'When he found out what I was, he couldn't wait to get out of here. He hightailed it back to New York on the next flight.'

Megan came to her feet. 'You mean—he abandoned you and Remy?'

'No.' Anita was honest. 'To give him his due, he didn't know I was pregnant when he left. But until then he'd been planning to take me back to meet his parents. He was a student, you see. He'd been working at one of the bars in Port Serrat during his summer break.'

'Oh, Anita!' Megan crossed the room and captured the other woman's hands and held them tightly. 'I'm so sorry. I know I keep saying that, but I don't know what else to say.' She bit her lip. 'Did you love him? Were you terribly distressed when he walked out?'

'I survived.' Anita grimaced. 'Pops was a great support, and when Remy was born I thought I was the luckiest girl in the world.' Her eyes glistened suddenly. 'I love that boy, Megan. I love him so much. I don't want anything like that to ever happen to him.'

Megan swallowed. 'Of course not.'

'Which is why I was so glad when he decided to come back to San Felipe when he'd finished college,' Anita continued. 'And now he has Rachel, and I don't have to worry any more. Her family—like most of the families on the island—has a mixed heritage. There's no danger of her accusing him of trying to ruin her life.'

Megan nodded, but she had the feeling there was a hidden message there for her, too. Anita might not know what had happened, but she had perhaps sensed a certain affinity between her son and her stepsister. Had Ryan sensed the same? Was that why he had wanted her to know the truth?

After a little while, Anita released herself, and, moving back to her chair, she extracted a tissue from her purse. 'So now you know all our little secrets,' she said, blowing her nose briskly. 'I hope it won't make any difference to the way you feel about us.'

'As if it could.' Megan was vehement. 'Anita, I'm ashamed of the way my father behaved. How could he, when he had spent so much time in Africa?'

'It's not important now.'

'It is to me.'

'Well...' Anita lifted her shoulders. 'I suppose he knew

there was no danger of becoming intimately involved with
his congregation,' she declared drily. 'It may even be one
of the reasons why he never took you with him. I imagine
it was something he fought against admitting, but when
your mother became involved with my father he couldn't
avoid it any more.'

'Yet he never said anything to me.'

'No.' Anita shrugged. 'Well, that's some consolation, I
suppose. Forget it, Megan. It's all in the past and we can't
do anything to change it.' She smiled. 'At least we're
friends, and, however your father felt, his prejudice can't
affect us.'

Megan hoped she was right, but she thought they were
both relieved when the waiter reappeared. 'Yes, Jules, you
can serve the meal now,' Anita told him. 'And then perhaps
you'd ask Michael to let me know when Dr O'Brien ar-
rives.'

'It's a bit late for the doctor to be making house calls,
isn't it?' Megan queried, after they were seated at the table
on the terrace, and Anita nodded.

'It's not exactly a house call,' she explained. 'Pops and
Doc O'Brien are old friends. Pops asked me to call him
earlier this evening. Like I said before, he was a little fe-
verish when I looked in on him, and O'Brien's visit will
calm him down.'

'I see.'

Megan accepted her explanation, but she couldn't help
worrying about the part she might have played in the old
man's possible relapse. He had shown some agitation when
he'd spoken of Remy, and she intended to reassure him
about that the next time they met.

In the event, the meal was over before Anita was called
away. Coffee had just been served, and Megan was wondering how soon she could make her excuses, when Jules
came back to say that Dr O'Brien had just arrived.

Anita departed at once, offering her apologies, and assuring Megan she'd see her again in the morning. 'Don't

worry about my father,' she added, as if sensing Megan's ambivalence. 'Believe me, he's tougher than he looks.'

Megan doubted that, but she bid her stepsister farewell, glad that she didn't have to manufacture an excuse for going up to her room. In the present circumstances, it would be so easy to give Anita the wrong impression, whereas her feelings for Remy were still the most troublesome thoughts she had.

Finishing her coffee, she left Anita's private apartments, and then trailed absently down the marble staircase to the ground floor. It was just a week since she'd arrived here, yet it seemed so much longer. So much had happened over which she'd had no control.

Not least, the development of her relationship with Remy, she acknowledged tensely, suddenly aware of his sensitivities as well as her own. Dear God, she thought in horror, did he think she'd known about his grandmother? Was he, even at this moment, labouring under the illusion that that was why she'd charged out of his apartment that afternoon?

She had to tell him, she thought frantically. She had to speak to him, and explain that until his mother had spoken to her she'd known nothing. She didn't know why it was so important that he should understand that she was innocent of any bias, but she was sure she'd never get to sleep until she'd done so.

There were several phones in the foyer, for the use of guests, and Megan stepped inside one of the plastic domes and picked up the receiver. She had no doubt she could have got Remy's number from one of the hotel receptionists, but she had no wish to alert Anita to what she was doing.

Which was why she was using one of the lobby phones instead of dialling from her own room, she admitted honestly, then the operator came on and she asked if she could give her the number of Mr Jeremy Robards' apartment in Moonraker's Yard. Despite the urgency that was driving her, she was not totally convinced that what she was doing

was entirely sensible, and the fewer people who were involved in her madness the better.

San Felipe wasn't a large island, and the four figure number was easily remembered. Finding a coin in her purse,
she dropped it into the slot and dialled the number she had
been given.

It seemed to ring for ages before it was answered and
she was just about to put down the receiver when the call
was connected. 'Yes?' said an impatient female voice that
she instantly recognised was Rachel's. And then, when
Megan didn't respond, she said, 'Remy, there's no one on
the line.'

Whether Remy himself would have taken charge of the
receiver at that point, Megan didn't wait to find out. Hurriedly replacing the hand-set, she stepped back from the
booth. She should have known Rachel would be there, she
chided herself bitterly. Her only consolation was that Remy
hadn't answered the phone himself and allowed her to make
a complete fool of herself.

Remy shifted restlessly between the sheets. It was after two
o'clock already, and he hadn't been to sleep yet. For the
past week, ever since he'd brought Megan to his apartment,
in fact, he'd had trouble sleeping, and he knew he was a
fool for not allowing Rachel to stay over.

But it would have been pointless inviting her to stay
feeling as he did. He could hardly tell her he didn't want
to sleep with her, and although he could make the excuse
that his restlessness would keep her awake that was only
part of the story.

However unlikely it seemed, the truth was that he no
longer wanted to make love with her. Although he'd known
her since before he'd gone away to college, and they'd been
dating constantly since he got back, the attraction was gone.
He'd tried to tell himself it was only a fleeting thing, that
as soon as Megan returned to England he'd get his life back
into perspective, but so far it wasn't working. On the con-

trary, Rachel had begun to irritate him, and he was having the devil's own job hiding his feelings.

Shifting onto his back, he gave up the unequal struggle and allowed the thoughts that were keeping him awake free rein. He was going to El Serrat tomorrow; his grandfather had requested to see him. And that was another source of frustration to him. The old man had never had to ask to see him before.

But what the hell was he supposed to do? If he went to the hotel, there was always the chance that he'd see Megan, and he'd made the decision to stay out of her way. In consequence, it was almost a week since he'd seen his grandfather, and his mother was constantly on his back, wanting to know what was going on.

He sighed and, pushing back the covers, he got out of bed. Perhaps if he made himself a drink it would help to cool his blood. Padding barefoot across the hall, he entered the kitchen via the living room, swinging open the fridge door and pulling out a carton of milk.

He drank deeply, wiping his mouth on the back of his hand when he was finished. Yeah, he thought, that was good. But it hadn't stopped him thinking about Megan, or the possibility of meeting her the following day.

He had to get some sleep. He'd promised to go and see the old man in the afternoon, but he had to work in the morning. The owners of an island cooperative wanted to sue their mainland distributor for undervaluing the weight of the sugar cane they had exported, and Remy was going to court to try and get an injunction to stop the man from moving the goods.

But, back in bed, his mind was as active as ever, and it was getting light before he fell into a fitful slumber. Even so, he was awake again before his alarm went off, and, pushing himself out of bed again, he went to take a shower.

The morning dragged. His client's case was at the end of the judge's list, and it was after two o'clock before he got back to his office. The fact that he'd pleaded his client's case successfully was some consolation, he supposed, and the men had been effusive with their thanks.

'You've got a pile of messages,' Sylvie advised him as he passed her desk on his way into his office. 'And your mother's called several times since twelve o'clock. Apparently, she was expecting you for lunch; is that right?'

'I said I'd try and make it,' Remy responded wearily, flicking through the pink slips she'd left on his desk. 'Most of these can wait, but you might ring a couple of the more urgent ones and explain the situation. Tell them I'll get back to them tomorrow.'

'Okay.' Sylvie had left her desk, and now stood with her shoulder against the door jamb. 'You look tired,' she commented drily. 'You should try an early night. At this rate, you'll be an old man before you're thirty.'

Remy regarded her sardonically. 'All I have are early nights,' he told her, dropping the pink slips back onto his desk.

'Then Miss De Vries must be stronger than she looks,' declared Sylvie irrepressibly, and, raising both hands, palms outwards, to ward off his retaliation, she shrugged her shoulders and went back to her desk.

If only it was that simple, thought Remy ruefully later that afternoon as he drove the few miles to El Serrat. He'd never had any real problem dealing with Rachel. They argued from time to time, but that was as far as it usually went. She'd certainly never disturbed his sleep, he reflected wryly as he swung round a bend in the road and the whole sweep of the bay lay ahead of him. Perhaps he took her for granted, he admitted honestly. Perhaps he always had, and that was why their relationship seemed so fragile now.

The russet-tiled roof of the hotel appeared below him, the road curving down in a delicate arc to the open gateway of Robards Reach. Avoiding meandering guests, he drove smoothly to the car park at the back of the building. Then, tossing his keys in one hand, he strode through the rear door into the foyer, acknowledging the porter's greeting before mounting the stairs to the first floor.

His mother was behind the reception desk, handling one of the guest's complaints personally. One of the reasons for the hotel's success was its boast that it gave a personal service, and there was no doubt that his mother was skilled in political diplomacy after all these years.

She registered his arrival with a faintly approving nod, but continued speaking to the man who had brought the complaint. She could have passed him over to one of the two female receptionists who were also present, but she didn't. In true Robards style, she herself made sure he was satisfied before he departed.

'Problems?' queried Remy as they passed through the door marked 'Private' and started down the hall towards his mother's sitting room.

'Just a misunderstanding,' she replied shortly. 'Room Service failed to deliver the exact meal he'd ordered last evening, and when he complained he felt the response was offhand. I'll have to speak to Lovelace. He'll know who was responsible. We can't have waiters who act as if they're doing the guests a favour by serving them.'

'Ah.'

Remy nodded, and, as if remembering why he was here, his mother gave him a disapproving look. 'You're late,' she commented as they entered the sitting room. 'You know lunch was at one. If you're hungry now, you'll have to make do with a sandwich, or have you already eaten?'

Remy went to help himself to a cool beer, twisting off the cap and taking a thirsty drink before replying. 'I haven't eaten,' he said at last, feeling grateful for having missed a possible family gathering. 'But don't worry. I'm not hungry. I just got out of court.'

'But it's almost three o'clock,' she protested, pausing in the doorway to the terrace. 'You must be hungry, Remy. You know it isn't wise to neglect these things. I hope Rachel will take more care of you when she moves in.'

Remy was glad she'd moved out onto the terrace as she was speaking and he wasn't obliged to make any reply. He dreaded to think what she'd say when he told her Rachel wasn't moving in with him. He knew she had her heart set on him settling down.

He followed her to the door, and found her hovering beside a pair of rattan chairs. 'Shall we sit out here?' she suggested. 'Your grandfather's asleep at the moment, and I haven't had a chance to talk to you for ages.'

'Okay.'

Remy took another swallow of his beer, and then sauntered across to join her in the shade of a striped canopy. From here it was possible to watch the activities on the beach, and admire the sails of the yachts that plied across the bay.

'So,' she said, when he'd stretched his length beside her, 'what have you been doing with yourself all week? I can't believe you've been so busy that you couldn't find time to visit your grandfather. He's a dying man, Remy, or have you forgotten?'

Her words stung. 'Of course I haven't forgotten,' he retorted. 'Dammit, Mom, I do have a job to do, you know.'

'And you've got a duty to your grandfather,' she countered. 'Without his help, you wouldn't be a lawyer. Don't you think you owe him a few minutes of your time?'

'But it's not just a few minutes of my time, is it?' Remy answered. 'It takes me a half hour to get out here to begin with, not to mention the time it takes to go back.' He sighed, because he knew he was only looking for excuses. 'I'm sorry, right? I'll do better from now on.'

'I'm pleased to hear it.' His mother looked a little less tight-lipped now, viewing his long, dark-suited legs with some sympathy. 'You came straight from the office,' she said, as if that had just occurred to her. 'I'm sorry, son. I don't mean to be so grumpy, but Pops has been driving me wild.'

'To see me?'

Remy was surprised, and his mother gave an impatient shake of her head. 'No, not that,' she said. 'That's a more recent demand. But he's had Doc O'Brien coming and going all week.'

'Why?' Remy was anxious. 'Has his condition deteriorated?'

'No, that's the annoying thing. Well, not annoying.' His mother was embarrassed. 'I just mean he's seemed brighter in recent days.'

'Well, that's good, isn't it?'

'Of course.' She gave him a chiding look. 'I suppose I've gotten used to letting Michael bear the burden. I suppose if it wasn't for Megan I'd have gotten no work done at all.'

Remy took another swig of his beer. 'Megan?' he said, when he was sure he had himself under control. 'Where does Megan come into it?'

'Oh, she's been helping me. It was your grandfather's idea to let her give me a hand in the office.'

'In the office?'

'Yes.' His mother looked rueful. 'I told him she's supposed to be relaxing, but there has been a lot to do. And what with Phoebe being sick and Tina leaving to get married—'

'I see.' Remy arched a dark eyebrow. It seemed as if his staying away hadn't meant a thing to Megan. Had she even noticed his absence? Or had she been far too busy playing the angel of mercy to give a thought to him?

'Anyway, I've no doubt she's been wondering why you haven't been around,' his mother continued, and he wondered somewhat guiltily if she'd read his thoughts. 'I told her that your evenings are usually tied up with Rachel, so I don't suppose she's been too concerned. And, of course, that young man of hers rings every other day.'

Remy's stomach muscles tightened. 'Simon?'

'Yes, that's his name.' His mother pulled a wry face. 'She insists he's just ringing about business matters, but I don't believe that.'

'Why not?'

'Why not?' She looked at him a little impatiently now. 'Remy, it's obvious the man's in love with her. Why else would he worry so much about how she is?'

'But is she in love with him?' murmured Remy thought-fully, and then adopted an innocent expression when his mother gave him a troubled look. 'Well,' he said defen-sively, 'she might have agreed to come out here to get away from him. Have you thought about that?'

'What disturbs me more is that you obviously have,' she retorted sharply. 'It's nothing to do with us, Remy. She'll be gone in a couple of weeks and I doubt if we'll see her again.'

'Why?'

'Why what?'

'Why do you doubt that we'll see her again?' He paused. 'I thought your inviting her here was to create a family reunion. Now you're talking as if you'll be glad when she leaves.'

'Well, perhaps I will.' His mother looked a little uncom-fortable now. 'I know I was eager to see her again, but it hasn't worked out exactly as I'd planned. Your grand-father's getting far too attached to her, for one thing, and for another I don't think she's happy here.'

'Why not?'

She frowned. 'Oh, I don't know.' She lifted her shoul-ders. 'She spends a lot of her time on her own. She went into Port Serrat last week and she wouldn't let me go with her. I was half afraid she'd gone there looking for you.'

Remy controlled his features with an effort. 'For me?' he echoed, managing to sound suitably surprised. 'Why should you think that?'

His mother sighed. 'Well—you must have noticed that she treats you more like her contemporary than me. That evening Rachel was here, I was quite embarrassed. Megan didn't say a lot, but she was watching you all the way through the meal.'

Remy's palms felt damp. 'You're imagining things,' he said, even as he acknowledged the fact that Megan had apparently kept their meeting to herself.

'I don't think so.' His mother was unconvinced. 'I think if you gave her the slightest encouragement she'd be happy to have an affair with you. But that's all it would be, believe me. She's her father's daughter as well. We mustn't forget that.'

Remy stared at her. 'What are you talking about?'

'I told her,' said his mother stiffly. And as Remy continued to hold her gaze she added, 'About your father; about your grandmother. Your grandfather wanted her to ask you about your father, but I thought it would be easier if I told her everything.'

Remy's throat felt dry. 'I see.' He stood his empty beer bottle on the ground beside him with exaggerated calmness. 'And what did she say?' he asked, with forced politeness, wondering if that was why she'd come looking for him in Port Serrat.

His mother shrugged. 'She was—surprised, I think. Shocked, even, though she didn't show it. But, as I said before, she is her father's daughter. Who knows what she's really thinking beneath that cool façade?'

Remy blew out a breath. 'But you think it upset her? That maybe that's why she—wanted to go to Port Serrat?'

'Oh, no.' His mother shook her head then, confounding him. 'She went to visit the cemetery, or so she said.'

Remy shifted forward in his seat, drawing up his knees and splaying his legs. 'So, when did she ask you about my father?' he enquired levelly. 'Was that before or after she made the trip?'

'Does it matter?' His mother looked at him strangely, and then, as if sensing his impatience, said, 'It was that evening, actually. The evening after she'd been to town. Your grandfather had been asking to see her all afternoon, and, as I say, it was he who told her to speak to you.'

Remy breathed deeply. 'She told you that, did she?'

'More or less.'

'What's that supposed to mean?'

'It means I asked her what your grandfather had said to her, if you must know. Pops was in quite a state when I went to see him. I was afraid she'd said something to upset him.'

Remy heaved a sigh. 'I see.'

'Anyway, it's as well to have these things out in the open,' declared his mother firmly. 'And I mean, I wasn't to know her father had never told her the truth. So far as she was concerned, she thought he'd taken exception to the fact that I was a young, unmarried mother. She had no idea there might be more to it than that.'

'And she was shocked,' said Remy flatly, watching her.

'Well, it was quite a surprise, I suppose.' She bit her lip. 'She was very sympathetic—about your father. But she couldn't really be anything else, could she?'

Couldn't she? Remy pressed his hands down on the sides of the chair, and got heavily to his feet. It wasn't unexpected, he supposed. He'd been anticipating her mentioning his background ever since she'd returned to the island. But, like his mother, he'd thought her father would have told her about his grandmother. He wondered how she'd react towards him now.

'How's Rachel?'

His mother's words forced him to answer her, though he doubted she'd like what he had to say. 'She's okay, I guess,' he replied. 'I haven't seen her for a few days.'

'Why not?'

'Because I haven't,' he said briefly, trying not to let his feelings show. He squared his shoulders. 'I guess it's time I went and saw the old man.'

CHAPTER TEN

MEGAN almost walked into Remy.

She'd been for a walk and her eyes were still dazzled from the glare of the sun on the water as she followed the shady path that led back to the hotel. It was quite late in the afternoon, but since she'd been giving Anita a hand with the bookkeeping it was often after four o'clock before she set out.

She hadn't known he was coming this afternoon, or she wouldn't have been out there. Anita hadn't told her he was expected, and he was the last person she'd anticipated meeting in the grounds of the hotel. This time she'd had no warning of the encounter, and it was an effort to meet his gaze with a neutral face.

'Hi,' he said softly, but there was something in his eyes that made her think he had been as reluctant to acknowledge her as she was him. There was constraint in his voice and a certain amount of resignation, as if he expected her to be nervous, and he wasn't disappointed.

'Hello,' she responded, her hand going automatically to her throat. Not that the scoop-necked vest was particularly revealing, apart from exposing a three-inch-wide band of flesh between its hem and her shorts. 'Are you here to see your grandfather?'

'Who else?' He was sardonic, and she wondered what he was thinking. Was he remembering what had happened at his apartment? Or had Rachel put such thoughts out of his head? 'It looks pretty hot out there.'

'It is.' Megan caught her lower lip between her teeth. 'I've been for a walk.'

'No sweat.' He acknowledged her admission without enthusiasm. 'Well, you be careful, Megan. We both know how debilitating the heat can be on pale skins.'

'Yes.' Megan felt her pulse quicken. 'I suppose you've been talking to your mother.'

'Right.' His eyes narrowed. 'But don't worry. I didn't tell her about your visit. As soon as I realised you hadn't mentioned it, I kept my big mouth shut.'

'Well, thanks. But that wasn't what I meant,' said Megan uncomfortably, aware that she shouldn't have said anything. 'Um—but it's probably just as well. In the circumstances.'

'Oh, yeah, the circumstances.' Remy's lips twisted. 'We mustn't forget them. D'you want to remind me which circumstances we're talking about? Just so I don't make a mistake.'

He was making fun of her. She knew it. And not gentle fun either. His was of a much more serious kind. She suspected he hadn't forgiven her for walking out of his apartment, but what else could she have done without losing her self-respect?

'Your mother wouldn't understand,' she declared now, aware that they were attracting unwelcome attention. 'You know how she feels about Rachel. I don't want to lose her friendship again. I don't want her to think I went to Port Serrat to—to see you.'

'You didn't?'

His brows arched, and Megan didn't know how to deal with him in this mood. 'No,' she insisted firmly. And then, she said, 'I never should have gone to your apartment.'

'Why not?' Remy regarded her enquiringly. 'We had lunch. What could she possibly object to about that?'

Megan's lips drew in. 'You're being deliberately obtuse.'

'Am I?'

'Yes.' She tilted her head defensively. 'You know your mother would never have approved of—of us being alone there.'

'Why not?'

'Because—because she wouldn't.' Megan lifted her

shoulders. 'I don't think she trusts me, if you want to know.'

A strange expression crossed Remy's face, and then he slumped back against the broad bole of the palm tree behind him. 'Perhaps it's you who doesn't trust me,' he suggested flatly, crossing his arms over the impressive width of his chest. His skin was dark against the white fabric, reminding her of what else his mother had said. Had Anita really told her because Ryan Robards had advised her to talk to Remy? Or was it just another attempt to drive them apart? 'That's why you don't want to talk about it.'

'There's nothing to talk about,' she said now, and would have moved past him if his hand hadn't closed about her arm.

'Perhaps you're ashamed of letting me touch you,' he commented harshly. 'Admit it, Megan, you're Giles Cross's daughter and we all know how he felt about my mother and me.'

Megan didn't even stop to consider her words then. Dragging her arm away from him, she faced him with contempt. 'That's a rotten thing to suggest!' she exclaimed, not even tempted to pretend she didn't understand. 'And it's not true.' She rubbed the red marks on her arm with trembling fingers. 'You're the one who should be ashamed. I hope Rachel realises what a faithless—oaf you are!'

It was hot in the sickroom; or perhaps it was only him, thought Remy disgustedly. He deserved to suffer the fires of hell—and probably would, he admitted—for behaving in the way he had. Dammit, he'd sworn to keep away from her, to avoid the kind of confrontation they'd just had. But seeing her again had seemed to addle his brain, and he hadn't been able to prevent himself from trying to make her squirm.

Only it hadn't worked that way. Instead of getting some satisfaction out of baiting her, all he'd done was frustrate himself. And destroy whatever communication there had been between them, he conceded bitterly.

Which didn't stop him wanting her at all...

His grandfather was awake and restless, his bony hands clenching and unclenching against the sheet. When he saw Remy, his eyes glittered with impatience, and he patted the bed beside him with obvious intent.

'Where've you been, boy?' he grunted, his breath whistling hoarsely in the still air. 'Don't tell me you haven't had time to come and see your old grandpa, 'cos I won't believe it.'

Remy perched on the side of the bed, loosening another button at his collar and pulling his tie partway down his chest. 'I have been working,' he said mildly, noting that the old man did seem more animated than usual. 'But I guess I've been neglecting you, too.'

'You better believe it.' Ryan Robards spoke with a surprisingly sharp edge to his voice. 'And you've been neglecting Laura—I mean Meggie,' he corrected himself hurriedly. 'I thought you liked the girl. Or is that useless hussy keeping you to herself?'

Remy doubted Rachel would appreciate being deemed a 'useless hussy', but his grandfather had always deplored the fact that she didn't have a job. He had worked all his life, and so had Remy's mother, and in Ryan's eyes a woman should want to help her man.

But it was the revealing use of Megan's mother's name that gave Remy most pause. His mother was right; his grandfather was becoming dangerously attached to Megan. So much so that he was beginning to confuse their names, and Remy was apprehensive of what would happen when she went back to England.

'I haven't seen much of Rachel, as it happens,' he remarked now, reminding himself that there had been nothing any of them could do for him before Megan arrived. 'Mom said you'd been asking to see me,' he added, avoiding her name. 'Was it just my pretty face you've been missing or have you got a problem?'

Ryan sighed. 'Did she tell you? Meggie, I mean. She comes and visits me every day.'

'That's good.' Remy endeavoured to sound enthusiastic. He forced a smile. 'I'm glad you get on so well.'

'Mmm.' His grandfather sought the relief of the oxygen mask, and breathed shallowly for several seconds before going on. 'I like her, Remy,' he wheezed at last. 'I like her a lot. She's exactly what this place needs: new life, new blood, new ideas—'

'Hold on—' Remy's hand closed over the old man's wrist in sudden consternation. He waited until he had his grandfather's attention, and then said carefully, 'She doesn't live here, Pops. I don't know what she's told you, but she's planning on going back to London in a couple of weeks.'

'I know that. Do you think I'm stupid?' The old man shook off his grandson's hand with unexpected strength. 'But perhaps she doesn't want to; perhaps she doesn't *have* to. Why shouldn't she have a stake in the hotel? It was her mother's home after all.'

Remy's jaw dropped. 'You're not serious!'

'Why not?'

'Why not?' Remy sought desperately for an answer. 'I—Mom would never go along with it. She's worked too hard for all these years to share it now.'

His grandfather fixed him with a milky gaze. 'Must I remind you that this is still *my* hotel?' he grunted harshly. 'I'm not dead yet, boy.'

Remy suppressed a groan. 'I know that,' he muttered awkwardly. 'But, dammit, Pops, the Crosses wanted no part of us.'

'Giles didn't,' agreed the old man grimly. 'He hated me, and I guess that's what killed him in the end. He couldn't bear the thought that he never forgave his wife. When she died any hope of his own redemption died with her.'

'Even so—'

'Meggie's not like her father,' Ryan persisted hoarsely, as if his grandson hadn't spoken. 'I know that. Anita's told her about your grandmother and she understands what Anita went through with your father. When we're talking together, I can almost pretend I've got Laura back again. Oh, I know what you think—what your mother probably thinks—that I'm getting senile. But I do know who Meggie is, and I think I know what she needs.'

'What she needs?' Remy stared at him. 'Pops, Megan doesn't need anything. She's a successful businesswoman in her own right, with a partner who might—' or might not, he chided himself mockingly '—be her lover as well.'

'He's not her lover,' said Ryan weakly, and Remy despised himself for the sudden leap of his pulse.

'How do you know?' he asked, belatedly realising how revealing his question was, and his grandfather's lips parted.

'Because he's not,' he declared doggedly. 'D'you think I wouldn't know? She's like her mother. She's open. She couldn't hide something like that from me.'

Remy's blood cooled. He should have known better, he thought disparagingly. For a minute there, he'd imagined Megan must have discussed her feelings with the old man. And he'd been stupid enough to expose his interest on the strength of nothing more than a hunch.

'Yeah, right,' he said now, getting up from the bed and pacing over to the window, forcing the slats of the blind apart and peering onto the verandah outside.

'You don't believe me, do you?'

The old man's voice was definitely frailer now, and Remy swung round with a determined smile. Dammit, what did it matter what he thought? His grandfather was dying. If it pleased him to leave a small share in the hotel to Megan, then why should his mother object?

But she would...

'If you say it's so, I believe you,' he said, approaching the bed again. 'But don't get your hopes up about Megan. She doesn't know squat about running a hotel.'

'She doesn't need to.' As his grandson's brows drew together Ryan panted, 'In any case, I told your mother to let her help out in the office. Anita's had to admit she's got a good head for figures.'

Remy blinked. 'Mom knows about this?'

'About what?' The old man could hardly get the words out, and Remy knew he shouldn't persist.

'About you—leaving Megan a share in the hotel?'

'Hell, no.' Ryan tried to laugh, but it came out as a winded chuckle. 'This is just between you and me, boy. What your mother doesn't know won't hurt her.'

Remy walked back to the hotel feeling uneasy. Not just because of what Ryan had told him, but because he was now obliged to face the consequences of what had happened earlier between him and Megan. It would be too much to hope that she'd stay out of his way until he was leaving. She despised him; he knew that. But she wouldn't back down from a fight.

He wondered if she knew what the old man was planning, and then immediately dismissed the thought. Whatever else Megan was, she wasn't dishonest. If she'd suspected what his grandfather had in mind, she would have mentioned it to his mother, he was sure.

In any case, it wasn't likely to happen. If the old man had asked to see his lawyer, he'd have been told. And his mother would have known and brought the subject up with him. His grandfather was probably playing a game with them all.

All the same, Remy couldn't help wondering what Megan would do if she inherited a part of the hotel. Would she keep it as an investment, or would she be prepared to sell it back to Anita if she asked? There was no way she would want to live on the island. Apart from anything else, she had another business to run.

His mother was in the lobby when he strolled into the hotel. She wouldn't admit that she'd been waiting for him, but it was obvious from her expression that she was expecting some explanation for the old man's insistence on seeing him.

'Well?' she said, when he joined her beside the flower-rimmed fountain. 'Is—is everything all right?'

'I guess.' Remy bent to pick a velvety-skinned magnolia from the display, smoothing its soft petals between his fingers. 'What do you think?'

'What do I think?' His mother set down the watering-can she had been wielding to give him an impatient look. 'You know what I think. I think he's becoming far too maudlin about the past. Encouraged—encouraged by Megan.'

Remy's lips thinned in resignation. 'You've really got it in for her, haven't you?' he protested. 'What grounds do you have for making an accusation like that?'

His mother snapped her fingers, ostensibly to get rid of the dampness that clung to their tips, but Remy sensed her frustration. 'I don't need grounds,' she declared irritably. 'I know your grandfather. I know what he's thinking. He thinks Megan is like her mother, but she's not. I loved Laura, you know I did, but Megan's *that man's* daughter. I thought it wouldn't matter, but it does. I should never have let your grandfather persuade me to get in touch with her. She doesn't belong here.'

Remy found himself shredding the magnolia, and thrust it back amongst the greenery. 'He doesn't think so,' he said shortly, looking with some distaste at his hands. 'Do you have a tissue?'

His mother supplied one almost automatically so that he could wipe the moisture from his fingers, but her mind was fixed on the remark he had made. 'He doesn't think so?' she echoed, and Remy cursed himself for giving her the opening she needed. 'What's that supposed to mean?'

Remy sighed. 'It doesn't matter.'

'It does matter.' Her eyes narrowed. 'Has he been saying something to you?' She stared at him suspiciously. 'You might as well tell me. I'll find out sooner or later.'

'Why don't you ask him?' retorted Remy, wishing he'd done as he'd told Megan he would and kept his big mouth shut. 'What he does is nothing to do with me—or you, for that matter.'

'You are joking.' His mother was incensed, and he

wished he could just turn away and leave. 'Let me guess,' she said harshly. 'He's trying to think of some way to keep her here, isn't he?'

Remy shrugged. 'I wouldn't know,' he said flatly, but his mother wasn't listening to him.

'That's it, isn't it?' she exclaimed, her eyes boring into his. 'He's going to try and bribe her, isn't he? How? By making you the prize?'

Remy was sickened by the suggestion, but his mother was triumphant. 'He thinks if he can dangle you like a carrot in front of her she'll stay—'

'No!' Remy couldn't let her go on thinking that. It was far too tempting a prospect. 'It's nothing to do with me. All right, I admit he wants her to stay. But I'm not the prize.'

'Then what is?' She swallowed convulsively. 'Not—not the hotel?'

Remy groaned. 'I don't want to talk about this—'

'So it is the hotel!' His mother's face had grown pale. 'No.' She shook her head. 'No, he wouldn't do that to me.'

'God, Mom—'

'I've worked too hard; I've sacrificed too much—'

'Stop it!' Remy couldn't stand much more of this. 'We all know how much you've given to the hotel, not least Pops, but is it so inconceivable that he should want to give the daughter of the woman he worshipped a small piece of it?'

His mother's mouth opened and closed, like a fish that had been too long out of water, and Remy was beginning to fear that she was having some kind of seizure when he saw Megan coming down the curved staircase. She obviously didn't expect to find them in the lobby, but it was the impetus he needed to bring his mother to her senses.

'Here's Megan,' he said, taking her arm, but as if his words were the final indignity she snatched her arm out of his grasp and hurried away towards the staff quarters, leaving him to offer whatever excuse he thought fit.

Perhaps Megan wouldn't have noticed them, he speculated later, if his mother hadn't made such an obvious exit. As it was, her hurrying footsteps were a dead give-away, and Megan's eyes registered her stepsister's departure with apparent concern before switching back to him in unmistakable accusation.

She seemed to hesitate, and he held his breath for a moment, willing her not to approach him, but when she reached the bottom step and turned in his direction he expelled his breath on a heavy sigh.

'What's wrong with Anita?' she asked in a puzzled voice, and he wondered if she had forgotten their altercation earlier.

'Who knows?' he responded, looking anywhere but at her. As if he didn't have a mirror-image of her slender, chemise-clad figure imprinted on his subconscious...

'You haven't—said anything to upset her, have you?' she ventured, and although he had warned himself not to let her provoke him the injustice of her words caught him on the raw.

'Such as what?' he enquired icily. 'What could I have possibly said to upset her?' He paused, and then added, unforgivably, 'Perhaps it wasn't me she was running away from.'

Megan's face paled. 'What do you mean?'

Remy fought back the urge to reassure her, and merely shrugged his shoulders. 'You tell me.'

Megan moistened her full lower lip, and for a moment he was mesmerised by the tantalising glimpse of her tongue. 'I can't,' she said unsteadily. 'I don't know what I've done.'

'Apart from looking like your mother, you mean?' he countered mockingly, and then, realising he was being unnecessarily cruel, he shook his head. 'Forget it,' he advised carelessly. 'She'll get over it. She always does.'

'Get over what?'

Megan was staring at him imploringly, and, realising he was in danger of saying too much, he looked ostentatiously at his watch. 'I've got to be going,' he said flatly. 'I've got someone to see at six o'clock.'

He turned away, but her voice arrested him. 'Remy.'

He stiffened without looking at her. 'What?'

'We need to talk,' she said, but he couldn't take any more.

'No, we don't,' he assured her harshly, and strode away through the swinging glass door.

CHAPTER ELEVEN

MEGAN decided to talk to Anita at dinnertime.

She wasn't looking forward to it, but she had to know what she was supposed to have done wrong. She'd spent the time since Remy's departure worrying about what he'd said and wishing she knew what was going on.

But when she arrived at Anita's apartments later that evening she discovered her stepsister wouldn't be joining her for dinner, after all. 'Mrs Robards has a headache,' the waiter who usually served them told her apologetically. 'Perhaps you'd eat in the restaurant this evening, Ms Cross. Mrs Robards says she'll see you in the morning.'

Megan sighed. She had no choice but to accept this explanation, but a headache sounded mightily convenient to her. She was fairly sure Anita was avoiding her, and she was tempted to storm into her bedroom and demand to know why she was being punished.

As she went down the stairs to the patio restaurant, however, she had to admit that during the last few days her relationship with Anita had changed. The warmth and affection she'd felt when she'd first arrived had been replaced with an impersonal politeness, and whenever she said she was going to see Ryan Anita often found an excuse why she shouldn't. He was sleeping, she'd say, or he'd just taken his medication—events that previously hadn't seemed important, but which now were offered as a reason why she should stay away from the sickroom.

But—foolishly, perhaps, she acknowledged now—she hadn't thought anything of it until that afternoon. Ryan had soon kicked up a fuss if Megan hadn't been to see him, and Anita had usually had to back down. She'd even attributed Anita's coolness to the worries she had about her father, remembering how anxious she had been about her own father when her mother died. Until that incident in the foyer, she'd assumed everything was all right.

After all, she hadn't hesitated in offering her help when Ryan had mentioned how overworked Anita was, and, working together in the office, she'd felt they'd found a certain rapport. It was only now she questioned her naïveté; in fact, Anita hadn't treated her any differently from any other of her employees. And there was no doubt that without Ryan's encouragement she would never have asked Megan for help.

Megan was given a table by the low wall overlooking the beach and the ocean. It was an excellent table, indicative of her status as stepdaughter of the proprietor, but she wasn't in the mood for such obsequious attention. She ate little—just a couple of shrimps and some grilled chicken—making her escape without waiting for coffee, and retreating to a stool in the Harbour Bar.

But even there she couldn't avoid the unwelcome advances of a man in striped biker shorts and a tank top, who evidently thought she had had a row with her boyfriend and was looking for company. Picking up her glass of mineral water, she sought refuge on the terrace, breathing a sigh of relief when her companion took the hint.

If only she knew what Remy had meant when he'd made that crack about her looking like her mother, she thought unhappily, sipping almost absently from her glass. One thing was certain, however—she couldn't ask his grandfather something like that. Despite the fact that she'd become surprisingly close to Ryan in the past couple of weeks, she wasn't foolish enough to think you could wipe away the effects of more than fifteen years in a few hours.

Nevertheless, it seemed obvious now that Anita resented it. But would that explain her behaviour this afternoon? What *had* Remy said to upset her? Why had he implied that his mother was running away?

Could he have told Anita about her visit to his apartment? she wondered. Although he'd denied having done so earlier, after their contretemps, she doubted he felt he owed her any favours. And he had seemed to imply that what she'd learned about his grandmother had affected her attitude towards him. He didn't seem to realise that her concerns lay in another direction entirely.

God! She shivered. If Anita resented her friendship with Ryan, she couldn't imagine how she'd feel if she discovered Megan was having a relationship with her son. And there was Rachel to consider as well—the young woman who evidently thought they were a couple. What the hell was Remy playing at? she fretted, feeling her eyes smarting with unshed tears. And why the hell did she care?

She'd go and phone Simon, she decided, finishing her mineral water. What she needed was his common sense right now. But then she remembered it was the middle of the night in England. Much as he cared for her, she doubted he'd appreciate being woken up because she felt blue.

She turned and rested her elbows on the rail behind her. Dinner was over now, and the terrace was becoming the haunt of romance-seekers, all wanting to enjoy the view. To see, but not be seen, she reflected enviously. It would be nice to share the rest of the evening with—with a friend.

She pushed away from the rail, and, depositing her empty glass on a nearby table, she left the terrace to the lovers. It was nearly nine o'clock; she supposed she could have an early night. The trouble was, she knew she wouldn't sleep, and her suite of rooms had never seemed less attractive.

She sauntered along the path that led round to the back of the hotel. It was quieter here, the people who were enjoying an after-dinner constitutional being bent on exercise and nothing more. The car park loomed ahead of her, mostly occupied by the vehicles used by the hotel staff. Few of Anita's employees actually lived in the hotel. Most of them drove in from the surrounding villages every morning.

An area at one end of the car park was used to accommodate the buggies. The small open-topped vehicles were a popular resource of the hotel. The one Megan had hired was there along with all its fellows, and as she approached the first she saw the keys still sitting in the ignition.

Her lips parted, and she glanced about her. It was a mistake, obviously. None of the other buggies had keys, as far as she could see. One of the guests must have borrowed the buggy, and forgotten to return the keys to Reception. Would anyone know if she took the car for a ride?

She didn't stop to find out. It was too good an opportunity to miss. She felt like a prisoner who'd just discovered her cell door was open. Being able to go out without first consulting Anita was too good to be true.

It wasn't until her headlights picked up the signpost that said 'You are now entering Port Serrat. Please drive carefully' that she paused to wonder exactly what she was doing. Until then, it had been enough to drive through the soft night air, with a velvety breeze brushing her temples, and the muted roar of the ocean in her ears. But now she had to face her own intentions; to acknowledge to herself precisely why she was here.

She'd just come for the drive, she defended herself. Where else could she have driven at this hour of the evening? If she'd taken one of the mountain roads that led to the interior of the island, she would have been foolhardy. Apart from the fact that they were narrow, she had no way of knowing whether they were made up or not.

She drove down towards the harbour, passing small houses where televisions flickered behind undrawn drapes. There were plenty of people about, but she guessed they were mostly tourists. There was a cruise ship in port, and its inhabitants were taking advantage of the duty-free shops.

She saw the narrow street she and Remy had taken to reach his apartment, and before she knew what she was doing she had turned into it and accelerated towards the alleyway that led to Moonraker's Yard. There were lights glittering in the archway and lamps burning in the courtyard beyond. She wondered if Remy was home, and if he was there with Rachel.

Stopping the buggy, she got out, still not acknowledging

to herself that this was really why she'd driven to Port Serrat. For heaven's sake, she chided herself impatiently, she was just curious about the area. Of course Rachel was with him. Where else was she likely to be?

But what if she wasn't?

The thought came out of nowhere, and although she tried to put it aside it was impossible to ignore. And who else could tell her why Anita was behaving so strangely? she asked herself reasonably. Even if Rachel was there, what did she have to lose?

Her dignity?

Her integrity?

Her self-respect?

The list was endless, but she refused to listen to any doubts. If Rachel was there, then she'd ask him to tell her what was going on and leave. If she wasn't... If Rachel wasn't there... Megan wet her lips. Oh, Lord, what did she really want?

Before she could change her mind, before she could get back into the buggy again and drive away, Megan hurried through the stone passage into the courtyard beyond. The steps were there, just as she remembered them, and she gripped the hand-rail as she climbed to the upper floor.

The studded wooden door was absurdly familiar. She'd only been here once before, yet she had no hesitation in identifying Remy's apartment. There was no bell, so she knocked, not without some trepidation, squeezing the buggy's keys between her fingers because she had nowhere else to put them.

Standing there, she made a bargain with her conscience. If Remy didn't answer at the first attempt, she'd go away. But he didn't, and she knocked again, bruising her knuckles. So much for her integrity, she thought, chewing her lower lip.

She was actually considering the merits of going away and finding a phone and ringing him when Remy opened the door. And, in consequence, although she'd believed she was prepared, she found she wasn't. Just seeing him again had the most profound effect on her, and the fact that he was only wearing a silk dressing gown caused an actual ache low in her stomach.

'Hello.' She spoke first, finding some relief for her emotions in breaking into words. 'Um—is Rachel here?'

It was a stupid question; she knew that at once. Of course Rachel was here. That was why Remy was only wearing a dressing gown. She had probably interrupted them, which was why he'd taken so long to come to the door.

Remy regarded her blankly. 'You want to see Rachel?' he said at last.

'I—why—no.' Megan was horribly embarrassed. 'I just thought she might be here. She—she was the last time I—I—'

She couldn't finish the sentence. How on earth could she explain that abortive call? But Remy wasn't so scrupulous. 'The last time you what?' he enquired silkily. 'Don't tell me you've come here before.'

'No! No, of course not.' Her face was flaming. 'Oh—if you must know, I phoned you. One evening.' She shifted uncomfortably. 'When Rachel answered, I disconnected the call.'

Remy's eyes darkened. 'So it was you,' he remarked. 'I wondered.'

'Well, you don't have to wonder any more,' said Megan, stepping back towards the staircase. 'I—er—I'm sorry I bothered you. Goodnight.'

'Wait!' Remy stepped forward, and she noticed he was barefoot, too. 'Rachel's not here, as it happens. I'm alone. As you've come so far, you might as well come in.'

Megan swallowed. 'She's not here?'

There was scepticism in her tone, and Remy's mouth turned down. 'No,' he said flatly. 'Why did you think she would be?' He glanced down at his robe-clad figure and grimaced. 'Oh, I see. Well, actually, I was taking a bath.'

'Oh!'

The relief in that small exclamation was revealing, but Megan was unaware of it. She was too busy noticing the

damp patches that spotted his gown. She saw now that the
cloth was clinging to his damp skin in places, and her
nerves prickled pleasantly as she stepped past him into the
hall.

Remy closed the door behind her, and because the hall
was too confining for them to conduct any kind of conversation there Megan did as she'd done before and walked
along to the living room.

Lamps were lit about the room giving it a warm ambi-
ence that was different from the last time she'd been here.
The curtains were not drawn, and she could see the lights
from the harbour below them, but it was dark tonight, and
the intimacy of her surroundings was enhanced.

Or perhaps it was only her, she thought ruefully. Certainly, there was nothing in Remy's expression at the moment to give her any hope that he might be pleased to see
her. On the contrary, he seemed suspicious of her appearance, and she surmised he wasn't making any guesses as
to why she'd come.

There was a pregnant silence while they each summed
one another up, and then Remy said, as if the invitation
was dragged from him, 'Can I offer you a drink?'

Megan licked her dry lips. 'Um—a Coke would be nice,'
she accepted gratefully, and he went past her into the
kitchen.

While he was gone, she looked about her, wondering
again what she was really doing here. What did she want
from him? What did she want from herself? A chance to
redeem their friendship, perhaps, but was that all?

'There you go.'

Remy had popped the cap on the can and poured half its
contents into a glass. He handed them both to her, his cool
fingers brushing lightly against her hot flesh, then he gestured to one of the squashy sofas, indicating that she should
sit down.

Megan didn't sit down. She took a thirsty gulp of the
ice-cold liquid, and then set both the can and the glass on
the stone rim of the hearth. 'That's good,' she said, straight-

ening and rubbing the palms of her hands together. 'Thanks.'

Remy folded his arms, his shoulders moving in a dismissive shrug. 'My pleasure.'

It was obvious he wasn't going to make this easy for her, and she wished she'd had a clearer idea of what she was going to say before she'd got here. To give herself time to think, she waved a hand towards the harbour lights behind her, and said, 'Doesn't it look pretty at night?'

Remy's lips took on a sardonic slant. 'Is that why you came?'

'What do you mean?'

'Well, I did suggest that you should come and see the view after dark,' he reminded her cynically. 'And I can't imagine any other reason why you might come here.'

'Can't you?'

It was an inflammatory thing to say, but Remy didn't take her up on it. 'No,' he replied flatly. 'I can't.' He waited a beat, and then continued with a twist of his lips, 'Does my mother know you're here?'

'Of course not,' she replied, and he arched a sardonic brow.

'Why "of course not"?' he queried drily. 'As I recall it, it was her opinion you were most concerned about this afternoon.'

'No one knows I'm here,' declared Megan, without answering him. 'I didn't even know I was coming here myself until I reached Port Serrat.'

Remy regarded her from beneath lowered lids. 'Is that supposed to be an excuse?' he enquired sardonically, and she gazed at him in sudden frustration.

'No,' she said. 'I'm just being honest with you, that's all.'

Remy snorted. 'That'll be a first.'

'I've never lied to you,' she protested.

'Haven't you?' Remy shrugged. 'Well, not in words, perhaps.'

Megan sighed. 'I didn't come here to argue with you,

Remy. And you should know that I could hardly ask your mother's permission to do anything. She's not even talking to me.'

'That's an exaggeration.'

'No, it's not.' Megan swallowed. 'She didn't even appear at dinnertime. She told Jules to tell me that she had a headache, but I don't believe she did.'

Remy shrugged. 'She does suffer from migraines from time to time,' he murmured mildly, but Megan wasn't having that.

'And I suppose it just came on as I was coming downstairs this afternoon,' she said sceptically. 'Come on, Remy; I wasn't born yesterday. I've done something—or she thinks I've done something,' she amended, her eyes flickering with unknowing hunger over his lean frame, 'and she's avoiding me. Isn't that the truth? You know it's so, so why don't you tell me what I'm supposed to have done?'

Remy lowered his arms, pushing his hands into the pockets of his robe. 'Have you considered that she might be jealous of you?' he asked, after a moment, and Megan's lips parted in sudden disbelief.

'Jealous of me?' she echoed. 'Why?'

Remy hesitated. 'Perhaps because the old man has taken such a fancy to you?' he suggested quietly. 'He has, you know.'

'Only because I remind him of my mother,' said Megan tersely, turning away so he couldn't see the pained expression in her eyes. 'Surely she doesn't begrudge me that?'

'Perhaps that's only a part of it,' murmured Remy softly, and she wondered if it was her imagination that made her think she could feel the warmth of his breath on the back of her neck.

'Only part of what?' she asked, chancing a glance over her shoulder, only to discover he had indeed closed the gap between them. 'I don't know what you mean.'

'Maybe the old man is hoping you'll change your mind about going back to London,' Remy offered lightly, and she was ashamed of the way her spirits plunged at his explanation. She realised she had been hoping for a more personal reason, and the knowledge that despite the fact that he was standing right behind her he had no intention of touching her caused her heart to plummet alarmingly.

'You must be wrong,' she said, turning sideways to avoid the impulse to lean back against him. 'It's like you said—he wants us to be friends. And we are. End of story.'

'What if he doesn't see it that way?' persisted Remy huskily, and he did touch her now, lifting a hand to tuck the silky strand of hair that had fallen across her cheek and hidden her profile from him behind her ear.

Megan shivered; she couldn't help herself. 'Well, he knows I've got to go back to London,' she said, a little breathlessly, and Remy's hand dropped to his side again.

'Because of—Simon?' he ventured evenly, and this time she didn't hesitate before giving her answer.

'No. Well—not in a personal way, anyway. He's my business partner.'

'Hmm.' Remy absorbed this, and she was intensely conscious of his eyes watching her. Then, without warning, he asked, 'Why did you phone me?'

Megan's breathing quickened. 'I—I can't remember now...'

Remy's mouth compressed. 'And you said you didn't lie,' he mocked.

'I don't—' Megan darted a glance sideways, and then wished she hadn't when she saw the resignation in his face. 'Well—it wasn't important,' she prevaricated. 'I just wanted to talk to you, that's all.'

'What about?' He was insistent and Megan closed her eyes.

'Oh—about what your mother had told me,' she admitted at last. She sighed. 'I wanted you to know that I hadn't known about your father before I—before I—'

'Walked out on me?' he suggested, and her eyes opened again.

'I suppose so.' She bent her head then, unknowingly exposing the vulnerable curve of her nape to his gaze. 'It was a stupid thing to do.'

'Walking out?' He gave a wryly amused laugh. 'Oh, I'd agree with you there.'

'No, I—' She turned to look at him, colouring at the sensual look in his eyes. 'That's not what I meant.'

'So you don't think it was stupid to walk out?'

Megan sighed. 'I meant it was stupid to phone you.'

'Why?'

'You know why.'

'Do I?'

'Rachel was here.'

'So?' He lifted his hand again and allowed his forefinger to trace a path from just below her ear to the corner of her mouth. 'Would it make any difference if I told you she left just after your call?' His thumb invaded her lips, tugging on the sensitive flesh. 'I wish I'd answered the call myself.'

Megan quivered. 'Why didn't you?'

'Well, it wasn't because I was struggling to get my clothes back on, if that's what you're thinking,' said Remy huskily, and she wondered if he could read her thoughts. He shrugged. 'Rachel beat me to it, that's all.'

'So what was she doing here?' asked Megan, and then realised it was really nothing to do with her.

But Remy didn't seem to mind. 'We'd had supper together,' he replied, his hand moving down to her throat and encircling the nape of her neck. 'We'd been talking about you, actually.'

Megan was amazed she could still get air past the tight muscles in her throat. 'What about me?' she asked thickly, aware of how easily this situation could get out of hand. 'I'm sure Rachel's not interested in me.'

'Did I say she was?' He caressed the soft flesh that bracketed the bony ridge of her spine, before allowing his hand to curve about her shoulder and draw her against him. He bent his head and kissed the skin exposed by the narrow straps of her dress, his tongue moving sensuously against her. 'But I think she realised how I felt.'

'Remy—'

'What?' His free hand tipped her face up to his. 'You want me to stop?' His hands fell away. 'Okay.'

Megan's tongue appeared between her lips. 'This isn't why I came here.'

'Isn't it?' His eyes darkened. 'I thought it was.'

Megan stiffened. 'You're making fun of me.'

'Of myself, perhaps,' he conceded tightly, taking one of her hands and bringing it to the heavy arousal that swelled against his robe. 'See what I mean?'

'Oh, Remy…' She couldn't help herself; she turned towards him, and his hands cupping her buttocks brought her fully against him. His thin dressing gown was no adequate barrier to the raw strength of his sex, and her legs went weak when he bent his head towards her.

He kissed her gently at first, lips parted, his tongue pushing wetly into the moist hollow of her mouth. There was an aching inevitability about it, she thought, as if he, as much as she herself, had no control over what he was doing. It seemed that ever since she'd come back to San Felipe they'd been heading for this moment, and this time Megan knew there was no turning back. She was past making excuses for what she now recognised was an irresistible attraction, and the possible outcome of what she was about to do was not something she was prepared to consider right now.

The kiss deepened and lengthened, his mouth seeking a more passionate connection as he felt her instinctive response. With something suspiciously like a groan, his hands spanned her waist, and she lifted her arms to wind them about his neck.

All she could think about was that he wanted her just as much as she wanted him. The powerful heat of his body wrapped itself around her, making her quiveringly aware of his need and hers, and of how much she wanted him inside her.

A steel band was playing somewhere down at the quayside, and the wild rhythm of the drums mingled with the erratic beat of her heart. A film of heat was making her whole body slick and unknowingly sexy, but it was nothing compared to the damp heat between her legs.

Remy kissed her many times, his mouth slanting across hers with ever increasing hunger, his teeth fastening greedily on her lower lip and reducing her to a helpless supplicant. Megan had never experienced such an onslaught on her emotions before, and she realised her relationships with other men had only been a poor imitation of the real thing.

When he drew back a little, she almost moaned in protest, but it was only to allow him to slip the straps of her chemise dress off her shoulders. The soft cotton pooled about her waist, exposing the lace-trimmed cups of her bra, and she felt a moan escape her when he bent to suck one of her nipples through the material.

Then, with a frankly sensual expression twisting his lips, he brought her hands down to release the catch of the bra before palming the swollen peaks. 'Does that feel good?' he asked huskily, and she could only nod rather frantically when he bent to suckle them again.

A feeling not unlike a shaft of pain shot from her breasts down into the pit of her stomach. A pulsing, tingling need spread down into her thighs, creating an actual ache between her legs, and as if sensing this Remy pushed her dress down over her hips and put his hand there.

Megan was trembling. She knew he must be able to feel how wet she was even through her silk panties, and she closed her eyes so he wouldn't be able to see the blatant hunger in them. She would never have believed she could come so close to losing what little control she had just because he was touching her, but she was.

His fingers were inside the leg of her panties now, inside her, and she couldn't help herself; she put her hands down and covered his. 'Please,' she begged, not knowing what else to say, and as if he understood how desperate she was he took his hand away, and swung her up into his arms.

His bedroom was across the hall, although she could not have described how they got there. With her arms tight around Remy's neck, and her face buried in his shoulder, she was only conscious of him and nothing else.

The quilt on his bed was cool at her back, but she hardly noticed. She felt as if her whole body was burning up, and when Remy peeled off his dressing gown and stretched his length beside her she moved convulsively into his embrace. Against her stomach, the throbbing heat of his erection was all she was aware of, and he slid her panties down her legs before raising himself to straddle her thighs.

She caught her breath then at the powerful length of him, rearing from a nest of curling dark hair, and as if sensing her sudden apprehension he paused. Keeping an admirable control on his own emotions, he smoothed the silky strands of hair back from her damp face, and brushed her lips with his thumbs.

'Are you sure about this?' he asked softly, and she marvelled at his sensitivity.

'I'm sure,' she breathed, not knowing how to tell him it was her own ability to please him that she was worried about, nothing more. 'Are you?'

'Oh, baby, I've never been so sure about anything in my life,' he assured her huskily, and, parting her legs, his fingers brought her to the brink of a climax she could only guess at.

Finally, his hands spread the blonde curls that marked the junction of her thighs, and then, with an ease of movement that was an innate part of his sexuality, he buried himself inside her. Her muscles swelled and expanded to accommodate him, but she was still half afraid she wouldn't be able to take all of him. Yet, somehow, she did, and the feeling of him filling her was like nothing she had ever felt before.

'Okay?' he asked in a hoarse voice, and she reached up to cup his face in her hands.

'Okay,' she agreed, pulling his mouth down to hers, and as he began to move she felt the ripples of her climax sweeping irrevocably over her. Her voice broke. 'I'm sorry...'

'Don't be.'

His thrusts quickened, and almost before the devastating effects of her first climax had ebbed she felt another coming right after it. This time, Remy joined her, and she was dizzily aware of his cry of release before his shuddering body collapsed in her arms…

CHAPTER TWELVE

MEGAN drove back to El Serrat in the early hours of the morning.

Remy had offered to drive her back but she'd insisted on going alone. The fewer people who knew where she'd been the better, she thought, and until she knew what they both wanted from this relationship she would rather keep it to herself.

'Besides,' she'd added huskily, when he'd protested that it was too late for her to be out alone, 'I'm already in enough trouble with your mother as it is.' She'd bestowed a soft kiss on the corner of his mouth. 'Can you imagine what her reaction would be if she discovered we'd been—together?'

'I don't particularly care,' said Remy thickly. 'She's going to find out sooner or later. But, if you insist—'

'I do.'

'Then when am I going to see you again?'

Megan caught her breath, her hands lingering on the hair-roughened skin exposed by the carelessly drawn lapels of his dressing gown. 'Soon, I hope,' she confessed, leaning towards him, and when Remy covered her open mouth with his it took an enormous effort of will on her part to pull herself away.

'You could always stay,' he said as she picked up her car keys and started for the door. He followed her down the steps to the courtyard in his bare feet. 'I'll phone my mother and tell her where you are. She can hardly change a *fait accompli*.'

Megan wished she felt as certain, but instead of answering him she tried to block his way. 'You'll get cold,' she said, pointing to his bare feet, but as the temperature still lurked somewhere in the mid-seventies Remy just gave her an old-fashioned look.

'You'll ring me when you get back?' he said, holding her upper arms in a possessive grip, and Megan nodded.

'I will,' she said, suddenly absurdly reluctant to leave the security he represented. She reached up to kiss him again. 'Until tomorrow, hmm? I'll be counting the hours.'

'I'll be counting the minutes,' Remy retorted roughly, letting her go with equal reluctance. 'Drive carefully.'

It was nearly two o'clock when Megan reached the hotel, but to her surprise the foyer was as brightly illuminated as it had been when she'd left. A station wagon she didn't recognise was parked at the door alongside another vehicle that she thought belonged to Dr O'Brien, and her guilty conscience immediately interpreted this as meaning that Anita had discovered her absence and had suffered some kind of collapse.

But then the more likely reason for Dr O'Brien to be here occurred to her, and her knees, which were already shaky, turned to water. Ryan, she thought sickly. Oh, God, was Ryan all right?

Instead of parking the buggy at the rear of the hotel where she'd found it, Megan abandoned it beside the other two vehicles and charged into the hotel. But despite the lights there didn't seem to be anyone about, and she was considering making the trek to Ryan's bungalow, to see if there were any lights on there, too, when Anita and two men, one of whom she didn't know, appeared at the top of the stairs.

Megan didn't know what to do. Anita's behaviour earlier that evening did not lead her to believe that her stepsister would be glad to see her, whatever the circumstances, and she half wished she could disappear as swiftly as Anita had done.

But to her surprise Anita didn't hesitate. As soon as she realised it was Megan who was standing in the foyer, she left the two men and hurried down the stairs towards her. 'Oh, Megan,' she choked, the tears streaming down her cheeks, 'he's gone. Pops is gone.' She enfolded the younger woman in her arms. 'He's dead! I just can't believe it's true.'

Megan could hardly believe it herself, but she was relieved that Anita didn't ask where she'd been. Nevertheless, she couldn't help feeling guilty. She should have been here, she thought unhappily. She should have been here for Anita's sake, if nothing else. Instead of which, she had been with Remy. She and Remy had been—

'Remy…'

She was hardly aware she had spoken his name out loud until Anita drew back to look at her. 'Oh, God, yes,' she said, dabbing her eyes with a tissue. 'I've got to tell Remy. He's going to be devastated when he hears the news. He and Pops—well, you know how close they were. If only he'd been at home when I phoned him earlier. I tried to reach him at his apartment and at his office, but I'm afraid he and Rachel must have been out with friends.'

Megan took an involuntary step backwards. 'You— phoned Remy?' she echoed faintly. 'When—when was that?'

'Does it matter?' Anita sniffed unhappily. 'It was earlier on, as I said. Half-past ten, maybe. What does it matter?'

Megan swallowed. Anita had not phoned at half-past ten. At half-past ten, she and Remy had been making love in his bedroom, with an extension of his phone on the table beside them…

But she couldn't tell Anita that, even though Anita's words troubled her quite a bit. Why would Remy's mother claim to have phoned her son when she hadn't? What could she possibly hope to gain by it?

'So—so when—?' Megan was amazed at how difficult it was to ask about Ryan's death. Yet, in the short time she'd known him, he had become incredibly important to her, and she knew his absence was going to make a difference.

'About eleven, I think.' Anita's breath caught in her throat. 'Sam—he was the nurse on duty tonight—called me about a quarter-past ten, when he noticed the monitor was—was—' She broke off, shaking her head helplessly. 'He tried, but there was nothing he could do; nothing anyone could do,' she added, giving way to another bout of tears, and Megan put a comforting arm about her shoulders.

The two men who had followed Anita down the stairs now approached, and Megan gave Dr O'Brien a sympathetic look. The doctor, who was not a young man himself, had known Ryan for a lot of years, and she guessed he must be feeling pretty bad about it himself.

'Megan,' he said, patting her shoulder, death creating a familiarity between all the participants somehow. 'This is a sorry occasion.'

Megan nodded. 'I know it sounds silly, but it—it was so sudden.'

'Hardly that,' said Anita sharply, recovering her composure. 'We've all been expecting it.'

'I think what Megan means is that Ryan had seemed a little better during the past few days,' declared O'Brien soothingly. 'I must admit, I was beginning to wonder if he wasn't going to confound us all.'

'You're not serious!' Anita dabbed her eyes with an impatient hand. 'You may have thought he was improving, but I thought he was trying to do too much.'

'Why?' O'Brien looked at her a little grimly now, and Megan wondered if she was only imagining the edge in his tone. 'You know Megan's being here had made a difference. Even you can't deny he gained a new lease of life when she arrived.'

'And much good it's done him,' retorted Anita coldly, causing the younger woman to catch her breath in sudden disbelief. She squared her shoulders, causing Megan's hand to fall to her side. 'I'm sorry. I can't help how I feel.'

Megan glanced at the doctor, the pain evident in her pale face, and he quickly drew the other man forward. 'This is Superintendent Lewis, Megan,' he said, to fill the awkward silence. 'From the Port Serrat Constabulary. He and I were having dinner together when I got Anita's call. Frank, this is Megan Cross. Mrs Robards' daughter.'

'How do you do?'

Megan managed to find the appropriate response, and the swarthy policeman gave her a rueful smile. 'Better than you at this moment, I should think,' he assured her gently. 'I'm so sorry we had to meet in such unhappy circumstances.'

'Megan's only been here a couple of weeks,' went on O'Brien, giving Anita time to compose herself. 'But you remember her mother, I'm sure.'

'Laura?' Superintendent Lewis's smile was warmer now. 'Oh, yes. I'm happy to say I knew your mother quite well, Miss Cross. I seem to remember meeting your father on one occasion, too.'

Megan nodded, and as if she'd decided that her stepsister had been the centre of attention long enough Anita intervened. 'An unforgettable encounter, I'm sure,' she said bitterly, and then, making an obvious effort to hide her resentment, she gestured towards the doors. 'And now, gentlemen, if you'll forgive me...'

'Of course, of course.'

It was Superintendent Lewis who instantly took the hint, but Dr O'Brien touched Megan's arm with curiously rueful fingers. 'You'll be all right?' he asked, and, guessing it was a covert reference to Anita's attitude, she gave him a determined nod.

'Someone—someone has to tell Remy,' she ventured, wondering if he might find it easier coming from someone other than his mother, but once again Anita broke in.

'I'm going to tell him,' she declared firmly, successfully dispensing with any offer the doctor might have made. She ushered the two men towards the door. 'He should be home by now. I'm going to drive into Port Serrat and tell him myself.'

'Oh, but—'

Megan started to make a protest, but one look from Anita was enough to silence her. And why not? she thought tensely. It was nothing to do with her. Not really. All right, she and Remy had become lovers, she couldn't deny that, but now that his grandfather was dead, who knew what it would mean to their relationship? What had Ryan said? That Remy knew where his real loyalties lay, that although he might rebel a little the hotel was his inheritance.

Tears pricked at the back of her eyes. Two weeks ago she'd have said that Ryan Robards' death would mean nothing to her, but it was true no longer. Curiously, he'd found his way into her affections and she'd miss their little tête-à-têtes more than she could say.

Because it seemed the polite thing to do, she accompanied the others to the door. She doubted she would get any sleep tonight anyway. She couldn't help thinking about Remy and what this was going to mean to him.

As soon as she saw the buggy at the door, she realised her mistake. Until then, Anita had forgotten to ask her why she'd been in the foyer at two o'clock in the morning, but now her eyes turned to Megan with evident intent. What was she thinking? Megan wondered anxiously. And what was she going to tell her if Anita asked where she'd been?

She couldn't tell her she'd been with Remy, she realised at once. Apart from anything else, it would be like charging Anita with lying about the call she was supposed to have made. Admitting she'd been at Remy's apartment since just after nine o'clock would be tantamount to an accusation, and, no matter how much she wanted to be honest about her relationship with Remy, now was not the time for confessions of that kind.

Nevertheless, she wasn't foolish enough to think that Anita wouldn't demand some explanation, and while her stepsister exchanged a final few words with Dr O'Brien Megan sought desperately for a solution. Somehow saying she couldn't sleep wouldn't cut it, and she decided she must be as honest as the circumstances allowed.

The two men were getting into their respective cars now, and Megan raised her hand in reluctant farewell. With Dr O'Brien's departure, the realisation that there really was nothing more any of them could do for Ryan struck her anew, and the tears that stung her eyes were as unexpected as they were profound.

She was smudging them away when Anita came towards her, her expression mirroring nothing but contempt. 'You've been out,' she said, and it wasn't a question. 'Where have you been?'

Megan drew a deep breath. 'I went for a drive,' she said honestly. 'I wasn't tired, so I thought you wouldn't mind if I borrowed one of the buggies.' She paused, and then, hoping to avoid any more questions, asked, 'How are you, by the way? If it's not a silly question, is your headache any better?'

'My headache?' If Megan had needed any proof that Anita's indisposition earlier had been manufactured, she had it then, but as if remembering what she'd told Jules to tell the younger woman Anita gave an impatient shake of her head. 'I haven't had time to think about it,' she declared tersely. 'Ever since Sam called to tell me Pops was—well, finding it difficult to breathe, I haven't had a moment to myself.'

'I know.' Megan felt guilty for doubting her. 'I'm so sorry, Anita.'

'I'll bet you are.'

The change in Anita's tone was startling, and Megan, who had been about to take her stepsister's arm in sympathy, stood back aghast. 'I beg your pardon?'

Anita shook her head, as if unwilling to get into any kind of argument now, and started off across the marble floor, but Megan had had enough of her insinuations.

'Anita!' she exclaimed, forcing her own emotions aside and going after her. 'Anita, what are you talking about? Why are you being like this?' She took an appalled breath. 'Are you implying that I had something to do with your father's death?'

Anita's shoulders heaved as she took a deep breath, and then, instead of starting up the stairs, she turned to face her. 'With his *death*?' she said harshly. 'Oh, no. I'm not implying you had anything to do with his death. You didn't want him to die, did you, Megan? He's no use to you dead!'

Megan gasped. 'I don't know what you mean!' she exclaimed in dismay. 'How—how could I—*use* your father?'

Anita snorted. 'To get a share of the hotel, of course,' she retorted contemptuously. 'It never occurred to me when I invited you here that you might see this place as some kind of an investment. Pops wanted to see you, he wanted to make his peace with you, and I, poor fool that I am, only wanted to please him. I never dreamt I might be inviting a—a snake into our midst!'

Megan was horrified. 'You're not serious!'

'Why not?'

'Why not?' Megan swallowed convulsively. 'Because it's not true.'

'You're telling me that you and Pops never discussed the hotel?'

'No.' Megan shook her head a little frantically. 'Of course we discussed the hotel. He—he was very proud of it. Why wouldn't we discuss it?'

'You're telling me you didn't put the idea of him leaving you a share in the hotel to him?'

'Of leaving me a share?' echoed Megan blankly, seemingly unable to do anything but repeat Anita's vile accusations. 'Of course I didn't put such an idea into his head.' She tried to think clearly. 'And it's not true. He hasn't left me a share of the hotel. You—you're imagining things.'

'I'm not imagining anything,' said Anita coldly. 'But you are if you think I'd let either of you get away with a thing like that.'

Megan was taken aback. 'I don't know what you're talking about,' she protested. 'Your father and I were friends. We had a friendship. There was no question of me—using him to get a part of the hotel. It's not mine. It's nothing to do with me. You have to believe me when I say—'

'Then why did Pops ask me to call Ben Dreyer?' demanded Anita fiercely. 'Ben Dreyer is his lawyer. He told me he wanted to speak to him tomorrow when I went to say goodnight.'

Megan's jaw sagged. 'I—I don't know,' she cried unsteadily. 'Did—did he say it was to do with me?'

'Oh, no.' Anita's lips twisted scornfully. 'No, he didn't say anything like that. He wouldn't tell me why he wanted to see him. But I'm not stupid! I knew what he had in mind.'

Megan quivered. 'Then it's just as well he died, isn't it?' she said tremulously, using the only defence she had. 'He's dead now, Anita. He won't be making any more calls on his lawyer. Your precious hotel's as safe as it ever was.'

Anita's face collapsed. One moment she was glaring at Megan, the hate she didn't attempt to hide shining in her eyes, and the next she had slumped down onto the lowest step of the staircase, burying her face in her hands, and giving way to noisy sobs. Rocking to and fro, her sturdy frame seeming to fall in upon itself, she had a pathetic appeal, and although Megan wanted to leave her her conscience was stirred.

'Anita,' she said desperately, sinking down beside the other woman and gathering her shuddering body into her arms. 'Oh, Anita, I wouldn't do anything to hurt you. Surely you know that?'

There was a moment when she thought Anita was going to reject her, when the plump shoulders stiffened, and it seemed as if she would pull away. But then the attraction of comfort apparently got the better of her, and she buried her face in Megan's shoulder and allowed the tears to flow.

CHAPTER THIRTEEN

MEGAN went to bed, but she didn't sleep. Despite the fact that she and Anita had ostensibly made their peace with one another, she knew she'd never forget the accusations her stepsister had made. Anita might have begged her forgiveness, she might have declared that she'd been distraught with grief, and that she hadn't known what she was saying, but Megan felt cold inside, and she doubted she'd ever feel warm again. She was hurt, frozen, numbed with the kind of chill that came from knowing herself betrayed. How could Anita have said those things? How could she have even thought them? Dear God, it was Anita who had invited her here. How could she believe that Megan had had anything more than Anita's father's well-being at heart?

But it was no use worrying about that now. As she crawled out of bed the next morning, Megan knew there were other problems to deal with, not least her relationship with Remy. How had he reacted to the news of his grandfather's death? Oh, Lord, she thought wearily, what was going to happen now?

She deliberately took a shower before getting dressed in an effort to revive her flagging spirits, and then slipped on a simple white tunic whose hem ended a modest couple of inches above her knees. She had become accustomed to not wearing make-up during the day, but this morning she felt obliged to apply a trace of blusher. Her drawn cheeks were waxen-pale, and she was sure she looked every inch her age, but no one could survive the kind of battering she had taken the night before without it showing in her face. She felt mentally, and physically, shattered, and she thought longingly of London and Simon's undemanding company.

Downstairs, the hotel was functioning as efficiently as usual, and Megan reflected, rather cynically, that Anita was unlikely to allow her father's death to interfere with her investment. Or was she being unnecessarily cruel? she wondered, realising that until the night before she hadn't really thought of Anita as being particularly ruthless. But she was, she acknowledged wryly. At least so far as the hotel was concerned, anyway.

Deciding she would rather not invade her stepsister's apartments until she was invited, Megan chose to take coffee in the lobby bar, seating herself by the window as she had done on her first morning here, when Remy had arrived to have breakfast with her.

Remy...

Sipping her coffee, Megan allowed thoughts other than those of her stepfather and stepsister to fill her subconscious, recalling the hours she had spent at Remy's apartment in glorious detail. Whatever the future held she knew she would never regret what had happened, and her memory of the way he had made her feel still caused a tingling sensation to spread throughout her whole body.

But then she remembered what had happened when she'd come back to the hotel, and the tingling sensation vanished. Oh, God, Ryan was dead. Dead! And although she hadn't said as much Megan knew Anita blamed her for that, as well.

She was still sitting there, with her empty coffee-cup in front of her, when she became aware of Remy crossing the foyer towards her. He was wearing a dark silk suit this morning, the whiteness of his shirt contrasting sharply with the tanned column of his throat. He looked heavy-eyed and weary, but so handsome that Megan felt her senses stir in spite of herself.

Yet, despite what had happened between them the night before, she was instantly aware of his relationship to Anita, and of the fact that the accusations his mother had made could just as easily have come from him.

'Hi,' he said, pulling out a chair and seating himself opposite her. 'I thought I might find you here.'

'Did you?' Megan was unaccountably nervous with him. 'I—I'm so sorry about your grandfather.' She caught her lower lip between her teeth. 'You must be devastated.'

'Well, sad, certainly,' he agreed gently. 'The old man was something else.' He lifted his shoulders. 'But it wasn't as if it was unexpected, despite the fact he'd appeared to rally these last few days. O'Brien was amazed he'd lasted as long as he had.'

'Was he?' Anita hadn't said that. 'Well, anyway, you have my condolences. He was a remarkable man.'

Remy's lips twisted. 'Your condolences?' he echoed softly. 'So formal. Why don't you just say we're all going to miss him? I am, and I guess you are, too.'

'What do you mean?'

Megan's response had been unnecessarily sharp, and Remy narrowed his eyes as he looked at her. 'What do I mean?' he asked mildly. 'What do you think I mean? You will miss him, won't you? Or were all those conversations you had with him just so much hot air?'

'No!' Megan was defensive, but she couldn't help it. After what Anita had said, she was sensitive to any hint that she might have had some ulterior motive for visiting Ryan. 'I—I liked your grandfather. A lot. But I realise my association with him can't compare to yours. Or your mother's.'

'Did I say it could?' Remy looked a little confused now. 'Come on, Megan. I know you got on well with the old man, and he was very fond of you.'

'Oh, I don't think—'

'He was,' Remy insisted flatly. He looked puzzled. 'Has someone implied he wasn't?'

'No.' Megan couldn't allow him to think that. To all intents and purposes, she and Anita had mended their differences. She had no desire to cause another rift by telling tales to her son. 'I just don't want you to think that I— well, that I imagine my relationship with him meant more to him than it did. We were friends. I reminded him of my mother. But that's all it was.'

Remy frowned. 'That sounds suspiciously like a defence to me,' he remarked drily. 'So—have I accused you of anything? If I have, then tell me about it. I don't want you to think I resent the affection that grew up between you and Pops. Hell, if seeing you made his last few days any easier, then I'm grateful. Okay?'

Megan swallowed. 'Okay.'

'Right.' Remy took a deep breath. 'So long as we understand one another.'

Megan nodded, but she couldn't help wondering how he would have felt if Ryan had decided to leave her a share of the hotel. It was all very well telling herself that Remy wasn't like his mother, but where money was concerned people could be surprisingly similar.

And, thinking of Anita, she said stiffly, 'Um—how is your mother this morning? She—er—she was pretty upset last night.'

'Yeah.' Remy pulled a wry face. 'I guess she was.' His eyes darkened. 'I gather she was waiting for you when you got back to the hotel.'

Now it was Megan's turn to draw a deep breath. 'Did she tell you that?'

'She said you turned up just as O'Brien was leaving,' he conceded levelly. 'She also said that you'd told her you'd been for a drive because you couldn't sleep.'

'That's right.' Megan pushed her cup aside, and, resting her forearms on the table, she twisted her hands together. Then, moistening her lips, she said, 'I could hardly tell her where I'd really been, could I?'

'Couldn't you?' Remy's response was a little more calculated now. But then, as if acknowledging that she had a point, he shrugged. 'I guess not.'

'Besides, it's not something I'd want to tell her,' went on Megan carefully, distinctly unwilling to mention the call Anita had claimed to have made. 'I mean, you know how she would feel if she knew, and—and until—until—'

'Until what?' Remy's tone had definitely hardened. 'Until the funeral is over? Until you decide what you want to do about it? Until you *leave?*'

'No.' Megan had never expected this kind of reaction. 'But, I mean, in the circumstances—'

'To hell with the circumstances,' said Remy harshly. 'I don't give a damn about the circumstances. Okay, Pops is dead, and no one's going to miss him more than me, but that doesn't mean I have to put my life on hold until my mother decides it's okay to start living again.'

'That's not what I meant.'

'Then what did you mean?' he asked, a dangerous edge to his voice. 'Okay, maybe this isn't the time to talk about it, but I'd like to know what you feel about it. About *us!*'

Megan swallowed again, uneasily aware of how exposed they were here, in the foyer, with his mother likely to come upon them at any moment. She wasn't afraid of Anita, she told herself fiercely, but she was afraid of what her words might do to their fragile relationship, and until Ryan was safely buried she didn't want to be the cause of any more friction between Anita and her family.

'You know how I feel,' she said now, in a low voice, but Remy's expression was not encouraging.

'Do I?'

'Yes.' Her palms were sweating and she pressed them tightly together. 'Last night—last night was—wonderful!'

'That's not exactly what I meant,' said Remy flatly. 'It was good sex—is that what you mean?'

'No—'

'It wasn't good sex?'

Megan sighed. 'You're deliberately misunderstanding me.'

'So tell me,' he urged, reaching across the table and covering her nervous hands with his. His thumbs massaged the vulnerable curve of her wrists. 'Tell me what it meant to you.'

'Oh, Remy—'

'That sounds better,' he approved, hearing the anguish in her voice. 'I like the way you say my name.'

'Remy—' She caught her lower lip between her teeth. 'We can't talk about this now. Not now.' She shook her head. 'I don't want to upset your mother any more than she already is—'

'But it's okay to upset me, right?' Remy smothered an oath and got abruptly to his feet. 'Forgive me; I was foolish enough to think that I was more important to you than my mother, but obviously I was wrong.' And, without another word, he strode away towards the stairs that led to his mother's apartments, taking them two at a time, and swiftly disappearing from her sight.

The funeral was held in the late afternoon.

Megan was amazed at the speed with which the arrangements had been made, but she understood the need for urgency in such a hot climate.

The service was held at the Baptist church in El Serrat, and she marvelled at the number of people who crammed into the small building. Most of the staff from the hotel were there, together with Ryan's sailing and drinking cronies from as far away as St Nicholas, at the north end of the island.

For her part, Megan stayed firmly in the background. Although she and Anita had spoken together briefly, she was still very much aware of feeling the outsider here, and she noticed that Remy kept firmly out of her way.

Which wasn't difficult, she conceded painfully, considering he was constantly surrounded by friends or Rachel's family. That young woman seemed permanently at his side, sharing the proffered condolences, consoling him in his grief.

Megan told herself she was glad. She wouldn't have wanted anyone to take too close a look at her eyes, which were red and puffy from the tears she had shed earlier. In fact, she had spent a good part of the morning crying, she thought tautly. For Ryan; for Anita; but mostly for Remy and herself.

As she stood at the back of the church, watching Remy as he gave his grandfather's eulogy, her heart swelled painfully in her chest. What if she'd caused an irreparable rift between them? she fretted anxiously. What if he refused to listen to her explanations? What if he decided he loved Rachel, after all? How would she survive?

It was dark by the time they got back from the cemetery in Port Serrat. Ryan had been laid to rest in the garden where his wife's ashes had been scattered, and Megan wondered fancifully if they were together again at last.

Anita had arranged for a buffet supper to be laid out on her private terrace, and several people, including Dr O'Brien, Superintendent Lewis, and Ben Dreyer, Ryan's lawyer, gathered about the tables. There was a small bar, and Megan noticed that Jules was on duty tonight, leaving Remy free to circulate among his fellow mourners. As before, Rachel was at his side, and, although Megan knew she could have joined Anita, once again she stayed in the background.

She was standing by the vine-hung trellis when she became aware of someone beside her. For a heart-stopping moment, she thought it was Remy, but a swift sideways glance disabused her of that thought. It was Dr O'Brien, and although she managed to summon up a faint smile she doubted he was deceived.

'I expect you'll be glad when it's all over,' he remarked, passing her a glass of wine. 'I know I will.' He grimaced. 'But it was a fine service. Ryan would have been pleased.'

Megan nodded, not trusting herself to speak, and as if understanding how she was feeling the doctor continued, 'Yes. And if it's any consolation he'd have wanted you to be here, too.'

'Would he?' The words were choked, and Megan cleared her throat before going on. 'I'm going to miss him.'

'Hmm.' O'Brien sipped his own wine with a thoughtful air. 'I know he was so pleased he'd made his peace with you at last. He and your mother—well, they loved you, you know.'

Megan looked down at her wine. 'I know.'

'And I'm sure Laura would have been glad to know that you're going to have a reason to come back to San Felipe now.'

'A reason?' Megan's brows drew together. 'Oh—you mean because the ice is broken at last?' She shook her head. 'It's nice of you to say so, but I doubt if I—'

'No. Not that.' The doctor interrupted her. 'I meant the hotel, of course.' He frowned. 'Ryan told you, didn't he?'

Megan's hand froze halfway to her mouth. 'Told me what?' she asked unsteadily, and O'Brien gave a muffled groan.

'Oh, God, he didn't, did he?' He pushed his thinning hair back with a troubled hand. 'I'm sorry, Megan. Hell, I forgot. He didn't have time to—' He broke off. 'He was going to tell you; he was. Dammit, why did I have to open my big mouth?'

Megan swallowed with some difficulty. 'You're not saying—' She distanced herself from him, mentally if not physically, and gave him a tormented look. 'I mean—Ryan didn't—he wouldn't—he hasn't—'

'Left you a piece of the hotel?' asked O'Brien heavily. 'Hell, yes. Of course he has.' And at her look of horror he added, 'Just a small piece.' He made a frustrated gesture. 'But for God's sake don't let Ben know I told you.'

Megan shook her head. 'But—I don't want it,' she protested, imagining how Anita was going to react when she discovered that her worst fears had been realised. Then, in a strained whisper, she asked, 'Are you sure?'

'Sure I'm sure.'

Megan wet her lips. 'But Anita—I mean, she mentioned that Ryan had—had asked to see his—his lawyer, but he was supposed to come today, wasn't he?'

The doctor snorted. 'I wonder how she came to tell you that?' he remarked drily. And then he said, 'Sure, Ryan had asked Ben to call, but it wasn't to change his will, if that's what Anita thought. He did that through me.' His lips twisted. 'He was a sly old beggar, right to the end.'

Megan felt sick. 'But why?' she asked a little wildly. 'Why would he do a thing like that? He—he doesn't owe me anything.'

'Perhaps because he wanted to,' said O'Brien quietly. 'I wasn't joking, Megan. He was very fond of you. And perhaps he wanted to ensure that you and Remy wouldn't lose touch with one another as you and he had.'

Megan put a trembling hand to her head, feeling the sweat beading on her forehead, the throbbing in her temples that warned of a headache to come. It couldn't be true, she told herself desperately. Ryan wouldn't leave her a share in the hotel. Dr O'Brien must be mistaken; he must have misunderstood. Ryan couldn't be so cruel, not knowing how Anita felt about Robards Reach.

'Are you all right?'

Remy's voice was like a cool breeze against her hot head, and although all day she had been dying for some indication that he had forgiven her for what had happened that morning she couldn't deal with him now.

'I'm—I'm fine,' she said, and she could hear the awful stiffness in her voice. 'Are you?'

Remy's dark eyes narrowed, and had she been watching she would have seen him exchange a speaking look with Dr O'Brien. 'I guess so,' he said evenly, and although she had sworn she couldn't cope with him her gaze darted irresistibly to his. 'I missed you earlier.'

'I think Megan's been keeping out of the way,' put in O'Brien, after a moment's awkward silence, and Remy frowned.

'Oh? Why?'

'Well, I imagine she thought you and your mother had your hands full as it was,' the doctor replied staunchly. 'Um—excuse me, won't you? I want to go and have a word with the Reverend.'

Remy inclined his head, but it was obvious his attention was focused elsewhere, and Megan wanted to weep at the thought of what he would think when he discovered what his grandfather had done. What his grandfather *was reputed to have done,* she amended fiercely, but there was really no doubt in her mind. Dr O'Brien wouldn't have said anything if he hadn't known it for a fact, and the idea that Remy might think she was as guilty of using his grandfather as his mother believed filled her with dread.

'Did you miss me?' he asked softly, and her bones melted at the tenderness in his voice. But she couldn't respond to it. Not now. Not with Ryan's will hanging, like the sword of Damocles, over her head.

'I—I liked the eulogy,' she said instead, seeing the light go out of his eyes. 'It—it was a beautiful service.'

'Yes, it was, wasn't it?' Remy took his cue from her, and adopted a cooler stance. 'I expect you're tired.'

'Pretty much,' she nodded, feeling as if she was dying inside. She glanced about her. 'Where's Rachel?'

She heard the oath he used then, even if it was barely audible. 'What is this, Megan?' he demanded harshly. 'What do you care where Rachel is?' His eyes glittered. 'You didn't give much thought to Rachel last night, as I remember.'

Megan's face flamed. 'I just thought—'

'Yes? What did you think?'

'Well—you have been with her all day.'

'I've been with lots of people,' he snarled angrily. 'And as you weren't willing for us to be together, then I don't think you can blame Rachel if she gets the wrong impression.'

Megan swayed back. 'I couldn't be with you,' she protested.

'Because you were afraid of what my mother might say?' he demanded, and when she gave a nervous little nod he acknowledged it with one of his own. 'Well, okay, I'll accept that. It probably wasn't the moment to get into that can of worms. But the funeral's over, Megan. You can't have any objections if I tell my mother I'm taking you back to town with me now—'

'No—'

She couldn't let him do it. Not until he knew exactly what his grandfather had done. How would she feel if he turned against her? It was not a prospect she even wanted to consider.

'Megan.'

His voice was anguished now, but there was nothing she could do. 'Just give me a little more time,' she begged, still hoping he might indulge her. 'I—I can't just walk out on your mother. If she needs me, I've got to be here for her.'

Remy closed his eyes for a moment, as if the sight of her offended his sensibilities, but when he opened them again all his anger had gone. Unfortunately, so had any emotion, she saw distractedly. His face was as cold as a mask.

'I thought you were different, Megan,' he said, and although the words were crippling there was no condemnation in his voice. 'But I was wrong. You don't want any commitment. What was I? Part of your cure? Or am I flattering myself? I was probably just a holiday romance.'

CHAPTER FOURTEEN

REMY swallowed the remainder of the beer in the bottle he was holding, and then set it down beside its fellows on his mother's coffee-table. There were, he saw with some disgust, at the least half a dozen empty bottles there already, and he was nowhere near as drunk as he wanted to be.

He shouldn't have accepted his mother's invitation to dinner, he acknowledged dourly. During the past month, he'd managed to avoid all her invitations, and although he knew that sooner or later he would have to deal with her for the time being he was better left to himself.

He wasn't in the mood for company—for any company, actually, but his mother's company in particular. His emotions were still too raw, too savage. It would take a lot of time for him to view her objectively again.

He needed another beer—or something stronger. Any minute now, his mother was going to join him. She was going to come into the room and expect him to behave towards her as he had always done, but he couldn't do it. Not without a stiffener, anyway, he conceded. Something to stop him from stuffing her invitation down her throat.

Realising he was getting dangerously maudlin, he got up from his chair and walked out onto the terrace. He had hoped to escape his thoughts in the darkness, but the sounds of music and laughter from the restaurant below only added to his misery. God, when was it going to get any easier? When was he going to accept the fact that Megan wasn't coming back?

He'd been so stupid, he realised bitterly. He'd thought that once the funeral was over, once his mother had come to terms with his grandfather's death, all he had to do was tell Megan how he felt. He had hoped that she'd understand

167

that the anger he'd shown towards her on the day of the funeral had only been frustration. And jealousy, he admitted honestly. He'd been jealous of the fact that she should put his mother's feelings before his.

But it hadn't worked like that, and he had only his mother to blame. As soon as she'd discovered that her father had left a ten per cent share in the hotel to Megan, she'd had hysterics, and by the time she'd calmed down Megan had been making arrangements to leave.

A corrosive pain twisted inside him as he recalled the frozen horror in Megan's face. He would never have believed his mother could behave so violently. She'd accused her stepsister of deception and collusion, and God knew what else besides.

It had all been so unnecessary. Pops had left her a forty-five per cent share of the hotel, for God's sake, so what was all the fuss about? It wasn't as if he'd made Megan part-owner. He'd left Remy the other forty-five per cent, which seemed eminently fair to him.

But his mother had been so blinded to anyone's feelings but her own that she hadn't cared that Megan was hurting. Remy was sure all she'd cared about was getting Megan out of the hotel, and no one would have wanted to stay in those circumstances.

All the same, he hadn't believed that Megan would leave without seeing him. When he'd left the hotel that night to go back to his apartment, he'd had every intention of coming back to see her the following day. But work had intervened, and it had been late in the evening when he'd arrived at El Serrat, only to find that Megan had left on the early evening flight.

Even then, he'd been sure she'd get in touch with him. He'd left word with Sylvie that if Miss Cross rang she was to be put through to him immediately. And if he was in court she'd had orders to get a message to him somehow. He'd had no intention of losing any opportunity to speak to Megan again.

But she hadn't rung, and when, after three agonising

weeks, he'd swallowed his pride and rung her, there'd been no reply. Well, not from her town house, at least, and he had no idea of the name of her company. His mother might have known it, but he'd had no wish to speak to her.

It was four weeks now, and the knowledge was killing him. Which was why he'd given in to his mother's pleas and come here tonight. He intended to ask her if she knew how he could get in touch with Megan. If it caused a row, so be it. After the way she'd screwed up his life, he didn't much care what she thought.

'Remy?'

He heard her voice now in the sitting room, and he guessed she was anxious in case he'd got bored and gone away. 'I'm here,' he said, shoving his hands into his trouser pockets and sauntering to the French doors. 'I was just getting some air.'

'I'm not surprised you need it.' Her voice was sharp at first, but then, as if realising she was walking on shaky ground, she bit her tongue. 'I'm sorry I've been so long. André is frantic. He's got ninety-five reservations for dinner, and he's having problems with two of the ovens.'

Remy shrugged. 'Tough.'

Anita's lips tightened. 'I might have known it wouldn't matter to you.' She squared her shoulders. 'When are you going to start showing some responsibility for the day-to-day running of the hotel? Your grandfather obviously expected us to work together.'

'I wonder if that's why he left Megan a share as a buffer?' Remy retorted, stepping into the room so that she could see his face. 'He knew we'd never agree on anything.'

'Yes.' Anita stiffened. 'Yes, well, that's what I wanted to talk to you about.' She bit her lip. 'I had word today from Ben Dreyer. Apparently, Megan wants to relinquish her share.'

'No!'

Remy's response was automatic, realising that if Megan gave up her share in the hotel he might never see her again.

'I'm afraid so.' His mother delicately pushed the empty

beer bottles aside, and set the vodka and tonic she had poured herself on the table. 'I know you don't want to believe it, Remy, but it does seem to vindicate my opinion. She's obviously had a guilty change of heart.'

Remy's lips twisted. 'You still believe you were right to accuse her of deluding the old man?' He shook his head. 'That's rubbish, and you know it. Pops never did anything without due care and consideration. He knew we'd never be able to work together without a mediator, so he gave Megan the deciding vote.'

Anita evidently didn't want to argue with him. 'Well, whatever the truth is, she doesn't want the responsibility,' she declared, taking a seat on the sofa. She patted the cushion beside her, looking up at him appealingly. 'Come on, darling. Sit down. Your grandfather wouldn't have wanted Giles Cross's daughter to come between us.'

'But she has come between us,' said Remy flatly, making no effort to join her. He moved to the bar and helped himself to another beer, despite his mother's mute look of disapproval. 'You might as well know, we were lovers. Only she was too afraid of offending you to admit it.'

Anita swallowed. 'I don't believe you.'

'It's true.'

'No.' Anita got to her feet. 'You're just saying this to hurt me.' She pressed her hands together. 'How can you be so cruel? You know that you and Rachel—'

'Rachel and I are finished,' Remy told her bleakly. 'We were finished the day I picked Megan up from the airport.'

Anita gasped. 'You're not serious.'

'I'm afraid I am.'

'But—but she's too old for you!'

'She said that, too.'

Anita's shoulders sagged in relief. 'There you are, then.'

'But it's not true,' Remy remarked evenly. 'Age has nothing to do with it.'

'You're saying that's not why she left you?' His mother's lip curled. 'Well, don't say I didn't warn you.'

'It wasn't anything to do with my grandmother either, if

that's what you're implying!' exclaimed Remy harshly. 'She left because you made it too unpleasant for her to stay.'

'So you say.'

'So I know,' retorted Remy, wishing he felt as certain as he sounded. 'In any case, that's why I'm here. I want to know the address of her company in England.'

'Her company?' Anita stared at him. 'Why?'

'Why?' Remy uttered a short laugh. 'Why do you think? Because I want to get in touch with her, of course.'

'But I've just told you, she wants to relinquish her share in the hotel.'

'So?'

'So, obviously she wants nothing more to do with us.'

'She wants nothing more to do with *you,*' Remy corrected her grimly. 'Megan and I—we have unfinished business.'

Anita pressed trembling hands to her lips. 'No.'

'Yes.'

'But you can't do this, Remy. Not now. Not now she's agreed to give up her share—'

'Agreed to?' Remy seized on the words. 'What do you mean, she *agreed* to give up her share? I thought you said Ben Dreyer had been in touch with you.'

Anita pushed back her hair with a nervous hand. 'Well, I did. He has. What I mean is—'

She was at a loss for words, and Remy saw it all now. Far from accepting the status quo, his mother had either contacted Megan, or had Ben Dreyer do it on her behalf, and asked her if she would be prepared to sell her share of the hotel. He felt sick with loathing. How could she? How could she do such a thing? To Megan, to his grandfather, to *him?*

'You—you—'

Words failed him now, and, as if sensing this might be her last chance to tell him her side of the story, Anita clutched his sleeve. 'Please,' she said. 'Please, Remy, listen to me. You know how ill your grandfather was, how frail.

People like that, people in that situation, are easily persuaded. Megan knew Pops confused her with Laura. She played on that, don't you see? Whatever she says about this directory of hers in London, it can't compare to this place. From the minute she got here, she must have been planning—'

'Shut up!'

Remy's words briefly silenced her, but when he pulled his arm out of her grasp she started again. 'You have to believe me, Remy. Goodness knows, everything I've done has been for you, for your heirs, for the children I thought you and Rachel were going to have—'

'I said shut up.' Remy couldn't stand any more of this. 'If you've done anything, it's been for yourself as much as anyone. My God, don't forget I know how devastated you were when I suggested Pops might want to leave Megan some small token—'

'A ten per cent share in a several-million-dollar enterprise is not a token,' snapped his mother angrily. 'I knew he was planning something. I just knew.' She twisted her hands together. 'But he was too clever for me. He knew when he asked to see Ben Dreyer that I'd think it was because he was going to change his will, but he'd already done it. By the time I heard about it, it was too late.'

Remy stiffened. 'Too late?' he echoed faintly. 'My God, you're not saying you had something to do with his sudden relapse?'

'No.' Anita looked horrified now. 'How can you even suggest such a thing? I loved your grandfather. I loved him very much. I'd never have done anything to hurt him.'

'But you have to admit his death was—unexpected.' He shook his head. 'My God, you didn't even have time to call me, to let me know—'

'I did call you,' said Anita at once. 'But you weren't there.'

'When?' Remy stared at her. 'When did you call me?'

'The—the night your grandfather died, of course.' Anita turned away. 'Must we talk about it now?'

'I was home the night Pops died,' said Remy grimly. 'If you'd called I'd have known about it.'

'How do you know?' Anita spread her hands. 'It's weeks ago now. How can you possibly remember where you were the night your grandfather died?'

'Because I was with Megan,' said Remy, not without some relish. 'If you must know, that was the night we became lovers. I wouldn't forget that.'

Anita's lips parted. 'Oh—well, maybe I got a wrong number—'

'Maybe you didn't,' said Remy harshly. 'You didn't phone me, did you? You deliberately didn't phone me. For God's sake, Mom, why?'

Anita seemed to shrink in upon herself. 'There was nothing you could have done,' she said, as she'd said so many times before. 'There was nothing anyone could do.'

'Maybe not, but—hell, Mom, what gave you the right to stop me from seeing Pops before he died?'

'If I'd known you were with Megan, I wouldn't have hesitated,' muttered Anita darkly. And then, as if she was weary of prevarication, she lifted her shoulders in a dismissive gesture. 'Oh, well, you might as well know, I suppose. I was afraid of what he might say to you.'

'To me?' Remy was confused. 'What about?'

'About his will, of course,' said Anita irritably. 'For pity's sake, Remy, I've just told you. I thought he was only *thinking* about changing his will. I didn't know he'd already done it.'

'And you thought if he told me what he was planning to do I might insist on giving Megan a part of my share, right?'

Anita nodded.

'Oh, Lord, Mom, does this place mean that much to you?' He groaned. 'You'd deny an old man's dying wish to ensure that you—'

'It wasn't his dying wish,' protested Anita tearfully. 'All he said was your name—and—and Megan's.'

'And from that you deduced that he wanted to trick you out of your inheritance?'

'Not him.' Anita licked her lips. 'Megan. Oh, Remy, say you forgive me. Say you won't hold this against me. I was only trying to do my best for—for us—'

'Not for us,' Remy told her coldly, feeling sick to his stomach. 'My God, no wonder Megan wanted to get out of here. She must think we're both—mad!'

'Does it matter what she thinks?' Anita went to him then, and in spite of his resistance she cupped his anguished face in her hands. 'Please, Remy, try to understand for my sake. I don't want that woman to ruin your life, as your father did mine.'

Remy couldn't help himself. He dashed her hands away and stepped back as if he couldn't bear for her to touch him. 'You know what, Mom?' he said bitterly. 'You're the only person who's ruined my life. I love Megan, and before all this happened I think she cared about me, too. But you destroyed that, just as surely as you've destroyed the one thing that might have brought her back to San Felipe. I'll never forgive you for that. Never.' He brushed past her then, feeling in desperate need of clean air. 'Excuse me, I think I'll take a rain check on that dinner, after all.'

CHAPTER FIFTEEN

THE plane had been late leaving London so it was after six o'clock when it touched down in San Felipe. Megan would have preferred the earlier arrival, not least because it would have given her some time to check into a hotel in Port Serrat before going in search of Remy, but as it was she was afraid that if she delayed any longer he might go out for the evening.

Of course, common sense told her to check into a hotel anyway—that whatever she had to say to Remy could be said just as easily the next morning—but her nerves wouldn't allow her to do that. Besides, she was very much afraid that if she waited until the next morning she wouldn't have the courage to beard Remy in his office, and once she had seen Ben Dreyer the temptation to leave without seeing him might overcome her instincts.

It probably wasn't the most sensible thing to see him anyway. It was over a month since she'd left San Felipe, and she hadn't heard a word from him since. Surely, if he'd wanted to see her again, if he'd had second thoughts about what he'd said to her the day of the funeral, he'd have made some effort to get in touch with her? But, although she'd waited expectantly for a call or a letter, she'd heard nothing.

It hadn't helped that Simon had been too wrapped up in his new relationship to spend any real time with her. The young man he'd told her about, the one who'd had such original ideas about introducing an ethnic section to the directory, had turned out to be more than a friend, and he and Simon had decided to set up house together.

Which meant Megan had had to find herself a new apartment. Naturally, Simon had wanted to sell his share of the house, and although he'd given her first refusal Megan had decided a completely new start would suit her better. In any case, the house was too big for one person, and Simon and Keith—she was rapidly getting used to the idea that they were a couple now—wanted to buy somewhere new, too. Keith had friends in another part of London, and Megan accepted that from now on Keith's wishes were going to figure large in Simon's plans.

Not that she objected to their relationship. On the contrary, she was glad Simon had found someone he could care for at last. One of the reasons they had decided to buy a house together was that he'd decided, after his last abortive affair, that he was unlikely to fall in love again, and she hoped Keith wouldn't let him down.

For her part, she had been having mixed feelings about her own future. Simon's contacts in Sydney had suggested that she might like to temporarily relocate there to organise an Australian directory, and she'd still been considering that when Anita's letter had arrived.

She shivered now, remembering how excited she'd been when she'd seen the San Felipe postmark, but Anita's missive had been short and to the point: as far as she was concerned, Megan had no real right to the share in the hotel Ryan Robards had left her, and as she was unlikely to find it of any intrinsic value Anita was offering to buy her out.

It was the final insult, but Megan was past caring what Anita thought of her any more. The scene she had created when her father's will had been read had destroyed any lingering affection Megan might have had for her, and gouged a rift between her and Remy that was so deep, she'd felt she had no choice but to leave the island at once.

Of course, when she'd got back to England, the situation hadn't seemed as clear-cut as it had done before. She'd realised then that she hadn't given Remy a chance to tell her how he felt about the situation, which was why she'd spent the last four weeks waiting anxiously for his call. But all that had arrived was Anita's letter, providing her with the opportunity to be free of the Robardses, once and for all.

Only her feelings wouldn't allow her to end it, just like that. She didn't want the share in the hotel, and she certainly didn't want Anita's money, but she did want to see Remy one last time, and a call to Ben Dreyer had given her the ideal excuse. There were papers to sign, papers which could have been dealt with by her solicitor, but which she had chosen to deal with herself. Which was why she was now riding in the back of a rackety cab, on her way to Port Serrat and Remy's apartment in Moonraker's Yard.

'Are you sure this is where you want to be, miss?'

While she had been musing over the circumstances that had brought her here, the taxi driver had stopped at the end of the alleyway that led into Remy's courtyard, and was peering somewhat doubtfully along the lamplit tunnel.

'Oh—yes. This is it,' she agreed hurriedly, pushing open the door and getting out, hauling the haversack, which was all she had brought, after her. 'How much?'

The driver stated the fare, and, using some of the dollars she had saved from the last time she was here, Megan paid him. 'Would you like me to wait?' he asked with a troubled frown, but Megan gave him a reassuring shake of her head.

'No. I'll be fine,' she said, stepping back from the cab. 'Thank you.'

The driver nodded, but she was aware of him waiting until she was safely through the alley before driving off. If only Remy would show as much consideration, she thought uneasily, climbing the stairs to the upper floor. *Oh, God, please don't let Rachel be here tonight.*

It wasn't until she had knocked at Remy's door that it occurred to her that he might be working late. Even though it was dark, it was only a little after seven o'clock, and she remembered how conscientious he had been. But someone was at home. She had barely acknowledged the possibility that Remy might be out before she heard the latch being lifted, and presently the door swung inwards.

Megan's legs went weak. No matter how eager she'd been to see him, the actual appearance of Remy in the open doorway briefly robbed her of speech. She'd anticipated this moment, longed for it, even, but now that she was really here she couldn't think of a thing to say.

It was partly due to the fact that he looked so stunned to see her, as if he'd never expected to see her again, and she didn't quite know what to make of that. Was his reaction due to a pleasurable disbelief, or was she really the last person he had wanted to see?

'Megan!' His use of her name was equally dazed. He gripped the back of his neck with a hand that she noticed wasn't quite steady. 'What—what are you doing here?'

Megan endeavoured to pull herself together. Forcing a lightness into her tone she was far from feeling, she managed to make a casual response. 'What do you think?'

'I don't know.'

Remy was wary, and as he moved into the light of the street lamp outside she saw how tired he looked. He had obviously been over-working, she thought anxiously, wondering if that was his way of dealing with his grandfather's death.

She hesitated, and then, deciding she had nothing to lose, she said, 'Aren't you going to invite me in?'

Remy seemed taken aback. 'Oh—of course,' he muttered stiffly, and, stepping back from the door, he allowed her to precede him down the hall.

The living room was a mess. Files and papers littered chairs and sofas alike, spilling onto the floor in places, and mingling with the various items of discarded clothing that were also strewn about. Significantly, several empty glasses occupied the captain's table, and there was the sweet-sour smell of alcohol in the air.

Megan paused just inside the doorway, appalled at the state of the room, and with a muffled oath Remy pushed past her. 'Sorry,' he said, stooping to gather up his papers from one of the sofas, and bundling several garments into a ball and depositing them in the kitchen. 'I wasn't expecting visitors.'

'No.'

Megan caught her lower lip between her teeth, more concerned by Remy's appearance than by the appearance of the room. Now that she could see him properly, she had noticed the days' growth of stubble that darkened his jawline, and the unfamiliar hollowness of his cheeks.

'I've been working at home today,' he added, gesturing to the sofa he'd cleared. His eyes flickered over the haversack she had dropped onto the floor. 'Can I get you something?'

Megan shook her head. 'Not right now, thanks.' She glanced about her. 'You've been busy.'

Remy's mouth twisted. 'You didn't come here to comment on my working practices,' he declared tersely. 'Did Sylvie send you?'

'Sylvie?'

Megan was confused, but Remy only heaved a resigned sigh. 'I assume you have been to the office first. Well, I have to tell you, it was nothing to do with me. I didn't even know my mother had contacted you until yesterday.'

Megan blinked, and then she realised what he was talking about. 'You think I've come about—about transferring my share in the hotel,' she said weakly. 'Well, no. I could have handled that by phone.'

Remy dropped the pile of files he was holding onto a chair, and regarded her with wary eyes. 'So why have you come here?' he asked. He frowned, and his eyes sought the haversack once more. 'Did you just arrive this afternoon?'

'This evening, actually,' said Megan, smoothing her damp palms down the seams of her jeans. 'The plane was late, so I came here directly from the airport.'

Remy's eyes narrowed, his thick lashes hiding their expression from her. 'To see me?' he said, as if he didn't believe it, and she gave a jerky nod. 'Why?'

Megan swallowed. 'You don't make it easy, do you?'

'What's that supposed to mean?'

'Well—' she lifted her shoulders in a helpless gesture '—I thought—I hoped—we might be able to iron out a few differences between us.'

Remy pushed his hands into the back pockets of the creased, but formal, trousers he was wearing, causing the unbuttoned neck of his shirt to gape. 'Like what?' he said, and although she had no reason to hope he would be any more understanding than his mother had been she had to try.

'Well, first of all, I want you to know I didn't have—have anything to do with your grandfather leaving me a share in the hotel.'

'I know that.'

Remy's tone was almost indifferent, and she could only gaze at him with wide, uncomprehending eyes. 'You know?'

'Sure.' He took a deep breath. 'I think I know you better than that.'

'Then why didn't you—?'

But she couldn't go on. How could she ask why he hadn't been in touch with her since she left the island? After what had happened at his grandfather's funeral, she had only herself to blame. If only she hadn't cared so much about Anita's feelings. If only she'd followed her heart instead of her head.

'Then why didn't I what?' he demanded now, and she realised he was waiting for her to finish. 'Try to persuade my mother that you had nothing to do with it?' he suggested. His mouth curled. 'Do you really think I didn't?'

Megan linked her hands together. 'But she didn't believe you?' she said, grateful for the diversion. 'I'm sorry she feels that way, but at least there's something I can do.'

'Yeah.' Remy took an involuntary step towards her, and she smelled the scent of alcohol on his breath. 'Reject the gift the old man wanted to give you,' he said harshly. 'Do you think that's what Pops would have wanted you to do?'

Megan breathed a little unevenly. 'It's what your mother wants me to do.'

'That's not what I asked.'

'Well, I—I assume it's what you want, too,' she said, shifting her weight from one foot to the other. 'But I'm glad you didn't think I'd—cheated you. And it's only fair that it should stay in—in the family.'

Remy's jaw compressed. 'The old man thought you were family,' he said, and she wondered how two people could stand so close without touching one another. 'He wanted you to have a reason to come to the island. He wanted us to stay in touch.'

Megan trembled. 'Us?' she ventured faintly. 'As in me and your mother?'

'No, *us*,' he muttered, seemingly unable to prevent himself from moving even closer. 'For God's sake, Megan, it was you and me he meant.'

Megan swayed, and, as if he was afraid she might fall, Remy wrenched his hands out of his trouser pockets and bracketed her shoulders between his palms. But he didn't pull her towards him or try to kiss her. He just held her there, as if he didn't trust himself to do more.

And, realising it was up to her to precipitate the situation, Megan lifted her hands and spread them against his chest. 'Don't you want me to give up my share of the hotel?' she asked in a tremulous whisper, and with a groan of anguish he gathered her into his arms.

'What I want…' he breathed against her neck, and she realised he was shaking '…what I want is for you to stop tormenting me.' He heaved a sigh. 'I swore I wouldn't do this. But, God help me, there's only so much a man can stand.'

Megan drew back to look into his haggard face. 'To stop tormenting you?' she breathed, cradling his face between her palms, feeling the prick of his beard against the pads of her fingers. 'Oh, Remy, I don't want to torment you. I'm here because I hoped you might still want me.'

'No.' His denial was harsh.

'No, you don't want me?' Her heart plummeted.

'No, I do,' he groaned, pulling her close to him again. 'But, dammit, Megan, it wasn't me who went away without even saying goodbye.'

'Oh…' The breath left her lungs with dizzying speed,

and she clung to him as if she'd never let him go. 'I—I thought you wouldn't want to see me,' she protested. 'After what your mother said, I—I had to get away.'

A sigh escaped him. 'But you didn't think of contacting me—'

'I'm here now.' She drew back and gave him a faintly defensive look. 'You didn't try to contact me either.'

'I did.' Remy lifted one hand to smooth back the moist tendrils of hair from her forehead. 'I tried to,' he amended. 'Eventually. But you were never at home.'

'Oh, God!' Megan gulped. 'I've moved out of the house I used to share with Simon. It's been empty for the past couple of weeks.'

Remy stared at her. 'You've split up?'

'Yes, we've split up.'

'Because of me?'

'No.' Megan saw the light go out of his eyes, and quickly reassured him. 'Because Simon's met a rather attractive young man called Keith,' she said softly. 'I did tell you we were only friends.'

'You didn't tell me he was gay,' said Remy huskily. 'Oh, God, you don't know the agonies I've suffered wondering if you were sharing a bed with him.'

'Simon and I have never shared a bed,' she assured him gently. 'But—' She coloured. 'I wouldn't say no if you—'

'Like this?' Remy held her face between his hands and glanced down at his rumpled appearance. Then, as if unable to stop himself, he bent and kissed her. 'Don't tempt me. I don't have much resistance right now.'

Megan quivered. 'I was hoping you'd say that,' she breathed, looping her arms about his neck. 'And I don't care how you look.'

'I do.' With slightly shaky hands, Remy put her away from him, and, taking a deep breath, started towards the door. 'Just give me time to take a shower and I'll begin to believe I'm human again.'

Remy had shaved the stubble from his chin, and was soaping his chest and body, when the shower door opened. He turned in amazement to find Megan stepping into the shower beside him, her lips curving into a smile when she saw his expression.

'I need a shower, too,' she said. 'I've just got off a long-haul flight. I didn't think you'd mind sharing. I can always rub your back, if you want.'

Remy shook his head. 'You know what I want,' he said, the sight of her causing an arousal he didn't attempt to hide. 'For God's sake, Megan, what are you doing? I haven't finished with the soap yet.' And then he said, in an anguished whisper, 'Oh, what the hell?'

He took her in his arms then, the soap sliding down unheeded between their wet bodies. Her mouth was moist and parted, her tongue darting to meet his with an eagerness he remembered from before. He'd never known a woman so instinctively attuned to his every need as Megan, and the feel of his erection against her flat stomach was the purest kind of torment he could imagine.

But the sweetest, too, he admitted, his tongue plunging eagerly into her mouth in frank imitation of what another part of his anatomy ached to do. 'God, Megan,' he breathed, 'I've nearly been out of my mind with wanting you.'

'Me, too,' she whispered, standing on tiptoe to nudge his swollen body with hers. She arched against him, and when his hands cupped her breasts, abrading the taut nipples, she groaned in protest.

'Megan,' he moaned, when she wound one of her legs about his thigh, unable to prevent himself from moving against her, and then, when she reached up to bite his lip, he lifted her completely, allowing her to wrap both her legs about his hips.

'This is crazy,' he choked, but already she was guiding his body into hers.

'Wonderfully crazy,' she agreed, covering his mouth with hers, and the feeling of her slick body accepting him was even better than he had imagined it. 'I love you,' she added, barely audibly, and her admission was all he needed to know...

Some time later, Megan stirred amid the tumbled covers of Remy's large bed. After he had made fast and furious love with her in his shower cubicle, they had retired to the more comfortable surroundings of his bedroom where, in this bed, he had made love to her again, this time with all the tenderness and sensitivity she could have wished.

'What time is it?' she murmured, finding him awake beside her, and he turned sleepy eyes towards the clock on the bedside cabinet.

'About half-past nine, I think,' he answered drowsily. 'Why? Are you hungry?'

'Only for you,' she answered mischievously, straddling him with one slim thigh. 'Oh, Remy, I'm so glad I came back.'

'So'm I,' he said huskily. 'I was beginning to think I'd only imagined that you felt the same way I did.'

'And how do you feel?' Megan traced the outline of his mouth with her forefinger. 'You never did tell me.'

'I haven't had a lot of time,' he replied ruefully. 'Besides, I thought I'd shown you.' His lips twisted. 'I love you. Of course I love you. As I told my mother, I think I fell in love with you that afternoon when I met you from the plane.'

Megan caught her breath. 'You told your mother?' She couldn't believe it.

He nodded. 'I told her we were lovers.'

'You didn't.'

'Yes, I did.' He gave a modest grin. 'She tried to tell me she'd phoned me the night Pops died, and I was able to state categorically that she couldn't have done or I'd have heard her.' He grimaced. 'Whether I'd have answered the phone is another matter.'

Megan's lips parted. 'She told me that, too.'

'She did?'

'Mmm.' Megan bit her lip. 'It was the night your grandfather died. I like to think I might have told her where I'd been if it hadn't been for the fact that I'd have been virtually calling her a liar.'

'She's called you a lot worse,' said Remy harshly. 'Oh, love! There have been so many misunderstandings.'

'But no more, hmm?' suggested Megan, bending to brush his throat with her tongue. Then she lifted her head, as if the thought had just occurred to her. 'Why did she say that anyway? Why would she say she'd phoned if she hadn't?'

Remy sighed. 'Well, I think the old man was still lucid when she got to him, and, according to her, he said both of our names.'

'So?' Megan frowned.

'Well—' Remy groaned. 'If you must know, the old man had hinted that he wanted to do something for you, and I was stupid enough to let her guess what he was thinking.'

'You don't mean—'

'Nothing disastrous,' he assured her gently. 'Just a fear on her part that if I got to speak to him Pops might tell me what he wanted to do.'

'But what did that matter?'

'She didn't know he'd already changed his will,' explained Remy. 'And she knew that if I'd heard what he wanted I'd have made sure his wishes were granted.'

Megan blinked. 'You'd have given me a piece of your share?'

'I guess,' he said in a low voice, and she snuggled her head into his shoulder.

'Oh, Remy!' She kissed him. 'Well, you can have my share now.'

'I don't want your share,' declared Remy firmly. 'The old man wanted you to have it, and unless you have some other reason for wanting rid of it, then I think you should keep it.'

Megan caught her breath. 'You don't mind?'

'For God's sake!' He was impatient. 'You never thought I did?'

'Well, your mother said—'

'My mother has a hell of a lot to answer for,' said Remy savagely. 'Megan, as far as I'm concerned you can keep your interest in the hotel with my blessing. In fact, I think you should.'

'But your mother—'

'My mother can hardly object if—if my wife owns a piece of the hotel,' he said evenly. 'That is, if this love you say you have for me encompasses marriage as well.'

Megan stared at him. 'You're proposing?'

Remy made a sardonic sound. 'It sounds like it.'

'Then in that case I might just keep my share,' she murmured teasingly. 'As a kind of reverse dowry.'

Remy scowled, pushing himself up onto his elbows. 'Does that mean you're accepting my proposal?' he asked, and she giggled.

'It sounds like it,' she said, turning his words back at him. 'I was looking for a new challenge. Helping to run a hotel sounds just the thing.'

And Remy's hoot of laughter as he bore her back into the pillows was a sign of his approval.

Nine months later, Anita's first grandchild was born.

It had been a busy nine months for Megan. First, there had been her marriage to Remy, and the exotic honeymoon they'd had in Fiji. Then a trip to England with her new husband, to transfer her share of the Chater-Cross Directory to Simon, and last, but not least, the discovery that she was pregnant, with all the excitement that entailed.

It had been a stressful time in some ways. Although Anita had been forced to accept her son's decision or risk losing contact with him altogether, she and Megan had taken some time to mend their differences. She very much resented Megan's involvement in the hotel, and there had been times when Megan feared they'd never come to terms.

Finding Megan was pregnant had made a difference. And Anita had had to concede that Remy had never looked so well. If Megan was responsible for that, she couldn't be all bad, she'd decided. And, as daughter-in-laws went, Megan was probably better than most.

For her part, Megan had found that being pregnant made her excessively tolerant, and now that she and Remy were married she could afford to overlook any little digs Anita might make. And, in time, they'd even come to an understanding, which the arrival of the newest member of the family could only endorse.

Megan's only regret was that Ryan wasn't there to see his great-grandson. And her mother, too, she reflected one sunny afternoon, when she and Remy wheeled their son's pushchair up to the cemetery.

'She'd have been so happy,' she whispered, feeling the security of her husband's arm about her as they sat in the Garden of Remembrance. 'Forgive me, Daddy, but I think the Robardses and the Crosses have made their peace at last.'

MILLS & BOON®

Next Month's Romances

Each month you can choose from a wide variety of romance novels from Mills & Boon®. Below are the new titles to look out for next month from the Presents™ and Enchanted™ series.

Presents™

FANTASY FOR TWO	Penny Jordan
AN EXCELLENT WIFE?	Charlotte Lamb
FUGITIVE BRIDE	Miranda Lee
THE GROOM SAID MAYBE!	Sandra Marton
THE MILLIONAIRE'S BABY	Diana Hamilton
MAKE-OVER MARRIAGE	Sharon Kendrick
THE SECRET FATHER	Kim Lawrence
WHEN DRAGONS DREAM	Kathleen O'Brien

Enchanted™

BERESFORD'S BRIDE	Margaret Way
THE FAKE FIANCÉ!	Leigh Michaels
A WEDDING IN THE FAMILY	Susan Fox
INSTANT MOTHER	Emma Richmond
RACHEL AND THE TOUGH GUY	Jeanne Allan
ANOTHER CHANCE FOR DADDY	Patricia Knoll
FALLING FOR JACK	Trisha David
MARRY IN HASTE	Heather Allison

On sale from 4th May 1998

H1 9804

Available at most branches of
**WH Smith, John Menzies, Martins, Tesco,
Asda, Volume One, Sainsbury and Safeway**

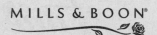

DANCE FEVER

How would you like to win a year's supply of Mills & Boon®
books? Well you can and they're FREE! Simply complete the
competition below and send it to us by 31st October 1998.
The first five correct entries picked after the closing date will
each win a year's subscription to the Mills & Boon series of
their choice. What could be easier?

OBLARMOL
AMBUR
RTOXTFO
RASQUE
GANCO

KOPLA
OOOOMTLCIN
MALOENCF
SITWT
LASSA

EVJI
TAZLW
ACHACH
SCDIO
MAABS

G	R	I	H	C	H	A	R	J	T	O	N
O	P	A	R	L	H	U	B	P	I	B	W
M	O	O	R	L	L	A	B	M	C	V	H
B	L	D	I	O	O	K	C	L	U	P	E
R	K	U	B	N	C	R	Q	H	V	R	Z
S	A	N	I	O	O	N	G	W	A	S	V
T	S	I	N	R	M	G	E	U	B	G	H
W	L	G	H	S	O	R	Q	M	M	B	L
I	A	P	N	O	T	S	L	R	A	H	C
S	S	L	U	K	I	A	S	F	S	L	S
T	O	R	T	X	O	F	O	X	T	R	F
G	U	I	P	Z	N	D	I	S	C	O	Q

D8C

Please turn over for details of how to enter ⇨

HOW TO ENTER

There is a list of fifteen mixed up words overleaf, all of which when unscrambled spell popular dances. When you have unscrambled each word, you will find them hidden in the grid. They may appear forwards, backwards or diagonally. As you find each one, draw a line through it. Find all fifteen and fill in the coupon below then pop this page into an envelope and post it today. Don't forget you could win a year's supply of Mills & Boon® books—you don't even need to pay for a stamp!

Mills & Boon Dance Fever Competition
FREEPOST CN81, Croydon, Surrey, CR9 3WZ
EIRE readers send competition to PO Box 4546, Dublin 24.

Please tick the series you would like to receive if you are one of the lucky winners

Presents™ ❏ Enchanted™ ❏ Medical Romance™ ❏
Historical Romance™ ❏ Temptation® ❏

Are you a Reader Service™ subscriber?   Yes ❏   No ❏

Ms/Mrs/Miss/Mr ....Intials ......(BLOCK CAPITALS PLEASE)

Surname..

Address ....

....

....Postcode..........................

(I am over 18 years of age)   D8C